HOT JOCKS 6

WILD
FOR YOU

New York Times & USA Today Bestselling Author
KENDALL RYAN

ABOUT THE BOOK

He's growly. Grumpy. Stubborn.

And now, my new roommate.

Walking away from my disastrous last relationship was an easy decision, but moving in with a friend-of-a-friend hockey star who's rarely home? Not quite as simple, because Grant makes me feel all kinds of things I'm not prepared for.

Protected. Desired. Unsteady.

• • •

She's beautiful. Smart. Tempting.

And a little fragile.

I've never been anyone's knight in shining armor, but when Ana needed a place to stay, it was easy to offer her a room with me.

Not so simple, though, is keeping my hands—or my mouth—to myself. And the night she crawls into my bed and shares her body with me? Heaven.

But she's not looking for a relationship, and to my surprise, I find myself pissed off by that idea.

They say my heart is broken, that I'll never settle down. I used to think that was true. Now, though? Hell, your guess is as good as mine.

First, she took my bed.

Then she took my heart.

Then she took my everything.

PLAYLIST

"New Vibe Who Dis" by Madison Mars feat. Little League

"Blame it On Me" by George Ezra

"Broken" by Lovely the band

"Higher Place" by Dimtri Vegas & Like Mike

"I Got U" by Duke Dumont

"Ride it" by Regard

"Fire on Fire" by Sam Smith

"Detlef Schrempf" by Band of Horses

"Kissing Strangers" by DNCE

CHAPTER ONE

Responsibilities

Grant

Being the captain of a pro hockey team comes with certain responsibilities. When I worked my ass off to become captain, I had no idea those responsibilities would include removing a monkey from a hot tub during a team trip to Thailand, searching for clothes for one of our forwards after he got locked out of a room by a puck bunny, and tonight, hunting down underwear for our newest defenseman.

Don't ask.

And now I've just completed another task, locating antacid tablets for our goalie's pregnant wife. There's never a dull moment.

"How's it hanging?" Jordie, one of the rookies,

asks when I re-enter the private dining room after handing over the antacids to Becca.

"Can't complain," I murmur, already scanning the room to locate my next project—the drunk left winger who's been a total pain in the ass tonight. *Shit*, to be honest, Jason Kress has been a pain in the ass since the moment he got traded here last year.

I spot him across the room, standing at the cash bar with a scowl on his face. His way-too-good-looking girlfriend stands nearby, talking to a couple of the other WAGs—wives and girlfriends—but I force my gaze away from her and focus back on Kress.

We're all here at the start-of-the-season banquet that our coaching team throws each year as a big preseason celebration before we head into the busy hockey season. All the wives and girlfriends are invited as a thanks for letting us steal their men for the next six months during the insane travel schedule hockey teams enjoy. I always come solo, though.

Most of the guys know to limit alcohol consumption at these events to one or two drinks. Apparently, Kress didn't get that memo. *Fucker.*

He's been an asshole all night. It's nothing I'd punch the guy in the face for, but he was short with his girlfriend and made some mocking remarks to her earlier. She looked miserable, and my stomach tightened in response. He's also drinking too much, and being loud and abrasive. It's enough that I noticed and felt bad for Ana, his girlfriend who moved from Las Vegas with him after he was traded to our team last year.

"Get me another beer," he says, loudly enough that I can hear him from my spot beside Jordie. "Ana, get me another fucking beer."

"Be right back," I say without taking my eyes off my target. Cursing under my breath, I approach the five-foot-eleven Kress, towering over him by several inches. "Haven't you had enough?"

"What are you, my sponsor?" He scoffs, rolling his eyes in my direction.

"I'm serious. Cool it," I say firmly. "Remember who you're representing. This isn't about getting shit-faced on free booze."

I've survived a dozen seasons as an ice hockey center, which means I've lived through ruthless training camps, injuries, and brutal playoff games. I'm known for my stamina and self-control, and performing under pressure. So for *this* to be my breaking point is, quite frankly, a little disappointing. I really didn't intend to lose my shit tonight. And at Jason Kress, no less.

Maybe I'm just getting too old for this shit.

Either way, I force a deep breath into my lungs, trying to calm the adrenaline coursing through my veins.

"Jason," his girlfriend says in a soft voice. Ana appears out of nowhere and touches his arm.

He shrugs aggressively out of her grasp. "Fuck this shit."

"Hey, time out," I say, stepping between them. "Kress, calm the fuck down."

He glares at us both. "You guys take a time out from being assholes."

"Kress . . ." Just as I open my mouth to reason with him, he storms away.

I expect him to sulk in the corner, or maybe sit down at the table where a couple of the other younger guys are enjoying a beer. Instead, he continues right on past everyone and out the doors, into the night air.

Ana looks visibly shaken beside me. I should say something, maybe offer some comfort, but small talk and emotions aren't exactly my forte.

"You okay?" I ask.

"Fine," she says, but I'm not sure she's telling the truth. Her full lips are turned down into a frown, and her hands are shaking.

I release a slow exhale and nod. I'm *definitely* getting too old for this shit. Since when did I become the dad of the team?

Ana mirrors my slow breath, but hers is more a shuddering exhale.

The fiancée of one of my best players puts her arm around Ana and guides her away. Good thing too, because I have absolutely no clue what's the right thing to say when someone's upset, which Ana obviously is.

Fuck.

"You guys good?" I ask when our goalie, Owen, and his pregnant wife, Becca, pass by.

They both nod, and Owen's hand moves protectively to her barely there belly.

After catching up with a couple of my teammates and talking with our coach, I spot Ana heading toward the side exit, a door I know leads to the hallway toward the kitchen. I know because I just came from there after hunting for the antacid.

"Here, have this." I hand my glass to Jordie. It's a warm, half-finished beer that I've been working on all night.

"Oh, you're so generous." He rolls his eyes.

"That's me, baby. Charitable." I smirk.

"Shut up."

"Okay," I mutter as I walk away.

Following Ana, I push open the door to the hall, but then stop short when I find her. She's slumped down against the wall, butt on the floor, knees up, arms folded around them, and her cheeks wet. When she spots me, she quickly wipes away her tears with the back of her hands.

Ana sits up a little straighter, and I clear my throat.

"Hey," I say, looking down at her small frame leaning against the wall. "You doing okay?"

Ana looks up, meeting my eyes. "I never should have come here," she murmurs, inhaling deeply.

Here to this party, or here to Seattle with her dickhead of a boyfriend? I'm not sure. Hell, maybe it's both.

I pull the handkerchief from my jacket pocket and offer it to her. "Please," I say when she hesitates. I never knew why suit jackets included those pocket squares, but maybe it's for this.

Finally, Ana accepts my offer, which is a relief because I have no idea what I'm doing. She dabs at her cheeks and eyes with the white cloth, and I think she's being demure until she brings it to her nose and blows—loudly. I smile, liking the fact she seems comfortable around me while I'm feeling anxious as fuck. Seriously, I don't do this shit.

"Thanks, Grant."

"It's all good." I wasn't even sure she knew my name, but I guess it makes sense that she does since I'm the team captain.

She's pretty, with those full lips and inquisitive brown eyes, and her cheeks have a rosy, youthful glow. Wisps of golden hair have escaped her low ponytail, framing her face, and her chest shudders with a huge, halting inhale.

God, she's so small. And she's shivering, I realize. Her slim shoulders are bare in the black spaghetti-strap dress she's wearing.

"Here," I say, shrugging out of my suit jacket, and bend down to wrap it around her slight frame.

"Thanks." Ana smiles up at me weakly.

Shifting my weight, I shove one hand in my pocket. *Say something, dude.* "Are you going to be all right?"

Okay, so it's not the most brilliant phrase I've ever uttered, but at least she's nodding.

"Yeah," she says, still looking up at me. "Jason gets in these moods sometimes, but he's mostly harmless." She stops herself and gives her head a little shake. "Sorry."

"Don't be." None of this is her fault. "Do you need a ride home?" I run one hand along the back of my neck, unsure of what I even want her answer to be.

She meets my eyes, seeming to weigh whatever it is she sees there. Seeming to determine if she can trust me.

Jesus. How did I get roped into this?

If I'd just minded my own damn business, none of this would have happened. It's really my beer's fault. If my beer hadn't been warm, I wouldn't have needed to refill it, and if I wouldn't have needed to refill it, I wouldn't have seen her rush off crying.

Crying females are my one weakness. Maybe it's because that's the only memory I have of my birth mother, before I was adopted by my parents. I remember sitting in her lap while her shoulders shook and tears fell in heavy drops from her eyes. To this day, I can't stand to see a woman cry.

"I can just get a ride, or call a car, or something. I promise, I'm not helpless." She wipes her nose one more time with my handkerchief, tucks it into her purse, and then rises to her feet. Once she's standing, she doesn't even clear my chin.

"I never said you were," I find myself saying, my gaze locked on hers. "But the offer still stands, and I'd prefer to know you got home safely."

Pulling in a big breath, Ana nods. "A ride would be great, actually."

"Sure thing."

We head back inside the private dining room and say good-bye to those still lingering around tables.

"Ana, call me tomorrow," more than one of the

girls say to her with a worried expression.

I'm wondering if they know something I don't. It sets off a feeling in my gut I don't particularly like. Clenching my hand into a fist, I take another deep breath.

Outside, I hand my ticket to the valet. Ana and I wait quietly side by side on the curb. I'm not one for small talk, but she doesn't seem bothered by this. Most woman chatter too much for my liking, but Ana is quiet too.

When my black sedan is pulled to the curb and the valet hops out, crossing around the front to open Ana's door, I'm momentarily dumbstruck. It's been years since I've been on anything even remotely resembling a date. And while this is most certainly not one either, it's the closest thing I've had in a long fucking time. I have a moment of uncertainty where I wonder if I'm supposed to be the one to open her door.

But it's too late. The valet beats me there, and then she's slipping inside the car.

I climb in too and watch as Ana fastens her seat belt. When I shift into drive, it occurs to me that I have no fucking idea where she and Kress live.

I clear my throat. "Where am I headed?"

Ana lets out a breathless sound. "Oh, right. Belltown. We live at Bell Street and Seventh. Little brick apartment building on the corner."

"Okay," I say, turning onto Bell.

"Thanks for doing this, Grant. I'm sorry again for any trouble I might have caused you."

"It's no trouble," I say, hoping she can't tell that's a lie. It is a little bit of trouble.

The last thing I want to do is get involved in a lover's quarrel when it involves one of the guys on my team. Especially considering that player is already a handful, without him being pissed off at me for getting in the middle of something I shouldn't have.

I take the turn onto Seventh and keep my eyes on the road ahead, and definitely not on the way Ana's dress slides up on her shapely thighs in the seat next to me.

"We're just about there," she says from beside me, waving one slender hand. "And then you can go back to whatever it is you had planned."

I can see her smiling from the corner of my eye. Smiling, like she knows something I don't. Smiling, like I had something planned for tonight besides sweatpants and sports highlights on the TV.

I pull to a stop at the corner, put the car into park, and turn to face her. She smiles at me. A warm, tender smile that I feel all the way down low in my stomach.

"Thank you again."

I frown and clear my throat, and her pretty smile falls. "Let me see your phone."

With an uncertain look, she reaches into her small clutch and produces a sleek smartphone.

I take it from her and program in my number. "This is my cell. Call me if you need anything, okay? No matter the time."

She hesitates for a second before accepting the phone back. "Okay." She slips out of my jacket and unbuckles the seat belt.

When I watch her climb from the car and walk away, I let out a huge breath and scrub my hands through my hair.

Okay. It's time to get home, get this suit off, and forget all about the gorgeous Ana.

And the fact that she's the first woman I've given my number to in years.

CHAPTER TWO

Tense Times

Ana

Digging my fingers into my client's skin, I seek out the knotted muscles I've come to know intimately. My thumbs work in unforgiving circles, knowing exactly how much pressure is just enough to keep Fred Winslow coming back for more every week. He groans on the table beneath me, a sign for this particular client that I should lighten up.

"You're in a mood today," the older man gasps out.

I feel that familiar flash of discomfort that I get whenever a stranger acts like he knows me. But I remind myself that he's a regular.

Some people prefer the anonymity of silence and professional distance, but this client is the kind who prefers to pretend he has a close relationship with his massage therapist. I know he sits at a desk for most of the day, managing databases for a car rental company. I know he sneaks yogurts both before and after dinner, much to his wife's annoyance.

I don't mind knowing these things. I just don't like him knowing anything about me, necessarily.

"And how is your mood today, Fred?" I ask, using my best massage therapist voice. It's low and buttery, like the voice my mother used when she'd snuggle under the covers with me to read a bedtime story. Sometimes it's spooky how much I sound like her.

"Oh, you know," he mumbles, barely audible against the table. "My wife thinks I need to cut out dairy . . ."

I only listen to Fred ramble as long as I need to, long enough to feel safe in my own thoughts. But Fred might be right. I suppose I am in a mood today. The banquet last night was a disaster. I knew it would be, since Jason had spent the afternoon griping about his life as a professional hockey player. And yet I still went.

"I'm not taken seriously," Jason growled, shoving his arms through the sleeves of his suit jacket as we were preparing to leave. "I know those fucking pricks talk about me behind my back."

"I'm sure that's not true. Why would you think that?" I asked, my voice slow and careful. I've learned to strip all emotion from my words when he's like this. If I'm hurt, then he's defensive. If I'm angry, then he's self-righteous. If I'm sad, then he's distant. It's a balancing act that I've never entirely mastered.

"What's that supposed to mean?" Jason turned back to me, shaking his head and glaring at me like I was an imbecile. "Don't ask stupid questions."

Don't ask stupid questions.

Fred winces beneath my touch, and I pull back, reentering reality.

"Uh, could you go a little lighter?" he asks kindly.

"Of course, Fred, I'm sorry. You've got some serious tension back here."

"It's sitting at that dang desk all day . . ."

After Fred leaves, it's already lunchtime. I see Georgia, the other female massage therapist at this hotel spa, waving at me from behind the glass windows of the hallway. We have lunch plans to walk down to the neighboring strip mall and eat at a Mexican-American fusion restaurant—a personal favorite of mine.

But my thoughts aren't on burrito bowls or potato-chip nachos . . . they're trapped on an endless repeat of last night's events. When Jason gets like that in public . . . well, I'm embarrassed and helpless, and nothing I say or do is ever the right thing.

Good thing Grant was there.

Since I moved to Seattle with Jason, I haven't spent too much time with the team, and certainly not with their huge, beast of a team captain, Grant, so he had no reason to check up on me or intervene at all. But he did, and I'll always be grateful. And then driving me home afterward . . . I should really send him flowers or something.

What do you send a wall of dense, sinewy muscle as a thank-you? A gym membership? Protein-packed chocolates?

After Georgia and I have placed our orders, we sit down across from each other at our favorite window booth. She frowns at me, her chin propped on two fists as she leans on the table with her elbows.

"Are you okay? You seem super quiet today."

I sigh. "I'm exhausted. The banquet was last night and—"

"Oh my God, right! How was that? I'm sorry, you were just about to tell me. I'll shut up. Go, go, speak." Georgia cringes and waves me on with one hand while using the other to pick up her fountain drink and take a long, occupying sip. We joke a lot about her inability to keep her motormouth from running, but it's nice to see her trying to control it. Emphasis on *trying*.

"It's okay." I giggle, finding myself in a much better mood. *Bless this woman.*

By the time our orders arrive at the table, I've filled Georgia in on the basics. Jason was in a shit mood all day, and he couldn't shake it off for the event. He got too drunk, made a complete ass of himself, and one of his teammates had to intervene. I got a ride home and spent most of the night waiting up, sick with worry, waiting for Jason to stumble back in, which he only did at four in the morning. When I got up this morning to get ready for work, he'd already left for practice.

"Jesus Christ!" Georgia blurts, unable to control herself. "I don't understand why he's like this. He's got a contract with one of the best teams in the league, he's making good money, and he's got an awesome girlfriend. What's his problem?"

I smirk at her compliment. "He's really hard on himself, so when he gets down like that, it's difficult for him to snap out of it. It usually escalates, especially when there's drinking involved," I say, parroting a mixture of what I've read online and my own justifications for staying with him.

Georgia reads my mind, because her next question echoes the very thoughts I couldn't shake last night, not long after Grant brought me home.

"Ana, babe. Do you really see a future with this guy? I'm sorry to ask, I just . . . I'm worried about you. I'm not convinced he's good for you." The little space between her eyebrows is creased with anxiety. "After hearing about last night, it's obvious."

I bite back my impulse to say something defensive, like, Why else would I be with him? Don't you think I have the emotional wherewithal to think about that?

But that's the difference between Jason and me. I can control myself and see things as they really are. Georgia is concerned, as she should be. She's my friend. She's just looking out for me.

"I don't know anymore," I hear myself say,

heaving out a slow breath. It's the first time I've ever admitted it out loud, and a chill of trepidation trickles down my spine. "Sometimes, I think about leaving and moving back home to be close to my dad. I could start over . . ."

When I pause, Georgia fills in the gaps like she always does.

"You'd rather run away than break up with him? I'm not a therapist, or at least a *brain* therapist," she says with a little smirk. "But I think that's a pretty big red flag."

I swallow, unsure of where this conversation is going. Is Georgia trying to tell me to break up with Jason? Is that what I want?

"Well," I say with a sigh, "as tired as I am of his tantrums, I've made my bed and I'm going to lie in it. At least until I decide what to do."

I dig into my lunch, a signal to the ever-perceptive Georgia that I'd rather not continue this conversation. My gaze is glued on rice, beans, and protein when I feel a hand touch mine. Georgia squeezes my fingers between hers.

"Okay, Ana. Just tell me if you ever feel unsafe. I'm with you through all of this. You might still think of Seattle as your new home, but it *is* your home, and you shouldn't be run out of here."

My chewing slows and I meet her eyes. "Thanks," I murmur through a mouthful of beans.

"And let me know if you ever need a massage. To alleviate some of that stress. Free of charge," she says brightly with a wink. "I know someone, and I've heard she has magical fingers."

I wash my food down with a cold gulp of water. We're always offering each other massages, but neither of us has taken the other up on it. It's just a simple way of saying *I love you* without really saying it.

"You too, Georgie."

• • •

That afternoon, my keys rattle in my hand as I struggle to open the door while holding leftovers from lunch and a small grocery bag in my arms.

After finishing my shift, I dropped by the market to grab some ingredients for white chocolate and pomegranate cookies—a specialty of mine. Baking always relaxes me, and after a stressful day, I need to relax. I can hear Hobbes whining from his kennel on the other side of the door.

"Coming, baby cakes," I call out. Hobbes is my Maltipoo mayhem machine, fondly named after the troublemaking stuffed tiger of comic strip fame. One of my mother's favorites, to be precise.

When I make it inside, I drop the food in the kitchen and immediately head for the kennel. When he's overexcited like this, I can't leave him alone for a second too long or he'll make a mess. I unlatch the kennel and Hobbes bursts out, running laps around the small one-bedroom apartment.

When I first moved here with Jason, he'd lost a lot of money in a bet. That catastrophe, paired with my own measly income, meant we could only afford something small. I actually prefer it. With the packed-to-the-brim bookshelves, secondhand furniture, and tight corners, our cozy little apartment reminds me of home. Or at least a slice of what life used to be.

I walk back to the door, coat and shoes still on, and call for Hobbes. He comes racing to me, jumping and twisting and showing me all of his tricks. It takes a moment for him to calm down, as it always does, but once the initial excitement to see me has passed, I can get him on the leash.

Out to the enclosed courtyard we go, just moments after another dog has left her own mark on the muddy ground. I unclasp Hobbes's leash, and he preoccupies himself with sniffing for a while before he ventures away to find his own patch of grass.

My thoughts wander back to last night, sitting in Grant's warm car as he drove me home. How he put his number in my phone, without any reason to believe that I'd use it.

Would I? If things ever got that bad, would I call the team captain? I can imagine how angry and hurt Jason would be if it ever came to that. How betrayed he'd feel.

As I watch Hobbes sniff around, it occurs to me that I shouldn't care about what Jason would think. If it ever came to calling Grant, it would be because Jason had majorly screwed up—like leaving me abandoned last night at the party. It's at this realization that I pull out my phone and send off a quick text to Grant.

> Hey, it's Ana. I just wanted to say thank you for the ride home last night. I hope it didn't cause you too much trouble. I appreciated it. Thanks again.

I consider adding a smiley face and then decide

that Grant doesn't exactly seem like an emoji type of guy. And if he was an emoji, he wouldn't be the smiley face. Though, I don't think there's one with a stern grimace and muscles everywhere. Smiling crookedly at that idea, I click SEND and shove the phone back in my pocket.

Hobbes scampers across the courtyard back to me, and I gather him in my arms. I'd rather not deal with the landlord sending yet another memo about mud tracked on the carpets of the communal areas.

I carry Hobbes inside, feeling his tiny little heartbeat racing from all that running around. I wonder momentarily if this is what I must look like to someone as giant and capable as Grant. Just a tiny little animal, unable to properly fend for herself in this big, bad world.

When my phone vibrates in my pocket, I pull it out. It's a text from Grant, consisting of one single word. I chuckle and shake my head.

Welcome.

Back inside the warmth of my apartment, I wipe Hobbes's paws with the towel I keep by the door and let him loose to pursue whatever shenanigans he's so eager to get into. In the kitchen, I roll up my sleeves and wash my hands, then I set the oven to 375 degrees and start making the cookie dough.

Flour, brown sugar, two eggs, a few drops of vanilla, and a pinch of salt . . . the methodical measuring of ingredients is calming to me. The tension in my shoulders begins to melt as the unsalted butter does the same, rising slightly above room temperature as I begin mixing. Oats and white chocolate chunks . . . comfort food.

I'm just about to start rolling the dough into little balls when I hear footsteps down the hall. My stomach clenches, which I know isn't the reaction I should have at the thought of my boyfriend arriving home.

Jason rattles the front doorknob, cursing loudly when he realizes it's locked. I stand in the kitchen, frozen. I could open the door for him, but my hands are all doughy.

"Ana!" Jason yells.

I jump, grasping my heart with flour-covered hands.

"Ana," he yells again, banging on the door. "I left my keys at the fucking rink. Let me in!"

I swallow as I hurry to wash my hands. Part of me imagines what it would be like to leave the door locked, wander to our room, and curl up in bed without Jason. The idea is more tempting than it should be, and the resulting guilt propels me toward the door.

"What took you so long?" he mutters, pushing past me when I let him inside. Hobbes growls from the corner, and Jason snaps at him. "Shut it."

It seems absolutely laughable that there was ever a time when I'd welcome Jason home with open arms, that he'd wrap me in a soft embrace and plant kisses on the top of my head. That was over a year ago, and so much has changed since then.

"I'm sorry," I say, training my voice once again. "I was in the kitchen and my hands were covered in gunk. I had to wash them first."

"Why does it smell like gas in here?" Jason asks, his voice more accusing than inquiring.

"I was making cookies."

"One of these days, I'm going to come home and you'll have burned the whole fucking building down." He sneers, dropping his hockey bag and coat on the floor as he heads for the bathroom. The door closes behind him.

I stay frozen to the spot until I hear the shower running. Hobbes plants himself outside the bathroom door, growling.

Like a zombie, I stumble back to the kitchen. It isn't until I place the cookie sheets into the oven with shaking hands that I realize how furious I am.

CHAPTER THREE

Broken Glass and Broken Promises

Grant

"I'm happy to go support the Little Rookies charity camp this year." I nod, opening the notebook I placed on the table in front of me.

"Great, so that's settled." Coach Dodd rests his elbows on the conference room table, looking around. "Choose another player to go with you too."

I grab the water bottle in front of me to take a long drink. We're halfway through our regular weekly meeting with the team leadership, the one I'm invited to sit in on as the team captain.

I write down the date for the charity camp event on the notebook calendar in front of me. The guys usually tease me, pointing out that there are more technology-friendly ways to keep track of my schedule, but today everyone's quiet. Maybe they're just focused on getting through the agenda that Coach has scrawled on the white board at one end of the conference room.

"What else?" Coach says, tapping his pen against the table as his gaze drifts to the agenda. "Oh, right, we need to decide which cause we're supporting this season."

Last year we supported breast cancer research, donating a portion of ticket sales to cancer treatment and awareness. Our usual black laces were replaced with pink ones in all the guys' skates last October.

"We need a decision in the next week. Grant, you got any suggestions?"

"Yeah," I reply, distracted as my cell phone vibrates in the pocket of my jeans. "Let me put some thought into it and get back to you by the end of the week."

"Sure thing," Coach Dodd says, then launches into the next agenda item as my phone vibrates again.

I pull it out and see a number I don't recognize. But based on the fact that whoever it is has called me twice in quick succession has my senses tingling and concern tightening my stomach.

"I need to take this," I say, holding up my phone.

Coach nods. "Sure, we're just wrapping up."

I slip out of my seat and head into the hall for some privacy as I answer. "Hello?"

"Grant." The woman's voice is a little breathless, and it takes me a second to place it.

"Ana?"

"Yeah, it's me. Sorry to call you out of the blue. It's just . . ."

An uncharacteristic feeling of worry stirs low in my gut. "It's fine. What's going on?"

She hesitates, and I hear her take a deep, steadying breath. "Can you, um, can you come get me?"

"Now?"

She hesitates again. "Yeah, if you could. But it's okay if you can't. I can figure something out."

"Where are you?"

"At the apartment. Second floor, 201."

"I'm on my way."

I end the call and stick my head back into the conference room to announce that I need to take off a few minutes early. Coach gives me a quick wave and says it's no problem. And then I'm on my way to the apartment where I dropped Ana off last night.

Honestly, I never expected her to be back here. Sure, I gave her my number just in case, but I never expected her to use it. Especially not so quickly.

In fifteen minutes, I'm back to the same corner I dropped Ana off at last night. But instead of stopping at the curb and keeping the engine running, this time I'm looking for parking. I locate a spot and leave my Tesla on the street, sticking out in this neighborhood like a sore thumb.

I make it up to the second floor and find the door to apartment 201 is open, just a crack. I take it as an invitation to enter, knocking twice as I push the door the rest of the way open.

"Kress? Ana?" I say, entering the space. It's empty, just a quiet foyer.

I have no idea if Jason is here, and if he is, I doubt my presence here would be welcome. I have the strong suspicion that his girlfriend texting me for help would be a huge problem, and the last thing

I need is to come to blows with my left winger in his own home.

We're cordial enough on the ice, but we're definitely not friendly away from hockey. First, I'd have to respect the guy, which I don't. And any idea of getting to know him outside of the team was destroyed by the asshole display he put on last night.

At first glance, you might think we have something in common. We're probably the two surliest bastards on the team, but the difference is—I know how to control my temper. I've never been the type to let my fists fly without pausing to think through the consequences. He gets into a lot of scuffles on the ice, whereas I only fight when absolutely necessary.

I hear a sniffle and then a distant voice.

"I'm in here."

As I follow Ana's voice and find her in the kitchen, I notice several things at once. The smell of something burning. Broken glass littering the tile floor as it crunches beneath my shoes. And Ana, crouched on the floor next to a cabinet with a smear of blood on the white tile at her feet.

"You're bleeding," I say, meeting her eyes

briefly. They aren't wet with tears like I expect. Instead, she looks embarrassed.

"I'm okay. I just stepped on some broken glass."

My expression hardens. "He do this?"

Ana nods. "He came home angry. We fought, and he threw a glass against the wall."

My gaze tracks up the wall where the force of the impact left shards of glass stuck into the drywall. It would have been about where Ana was standing before she sank to her spot on the floor.

Son of a bitch. He didn't throw a glass at the wall . . . he threw it at her head.

My fists clench at my sides. Kress has at least a hundred pounds on her. On what fucking planet does he think it's okay to treat his girl this way? To treat *anyone* this way? Let alone someone he should lay down his life to protect, care for, and . . .

A bark comes from somewhere deeper inside the apartment, interrupting my thoughts. But it's not the bark of a guard dog, which is too bad. A guard dog might have done something to protect her. No, it's the high-pitched yip of a lap dog. Maybe she locked it someplace for safekeeping while

Kress went on his rampage.

Since I don't do feelings, I go into captain mode, lifting Ana from the floor and setting her on the counter. Her bare feet dangle, one cut and bleeding.

"Where is your first aid kit?"

"I'm fine. It doesn't even hurt."

That's the adrenaline talking. She'll retract that statement as soon as she tries to put weight on it.

I meet her eyes. "I need to make sure there's no glass inside the wound. Where is your first aid kit?"

She nods and then points down the hall. "In the bathroom cabinet."

I have no idea where Kress is, or when he might be returning, but I focus on one thing at a time. Behind a box of feminine pads, I locate a first aid kit and carry it back to the kitchen.

Working methodically, I clean the wound and dress it in a light bandage. Ana stays quiet, watching me as I work.

"As far as I can tell there's no glass in it, and it's not deep enough to need stitches. But it'll be tender for a few days, and you should avoid putting too much weight on it."

She nods, her eyes watering as she stares back at me. "Thanks, Grant. I'm sorry, I didn't know who else to call. My friend Georgia didn't answer her phone, and I don't know many other people I trust enough to come here, and who know what Jason is like."

She doesn't need to apologize. When I gave her my number, I was serious about her using it if she needed something, but didn't expect it to be so soon—or to be for something like this. I'm just glad I didn't walk in to find her . . . *Fuck*, I couldn't even think of that.

"Has he done this before?" My voice comes out stern, and her gaze drops to the floor. "Ana, talk to me."

She doesn't reply, just keeps her eyes down and tries not to cry.

Fuck.

I take a deep breath, trying desperately to control my need to unleash hell on something or someone.

Fuck Jason. Fuck any man or woman who hurts

the person they're meant to protect. *Fuck!*

I shove the unused items back inside the first aid kit, snapping the plastic lid closed while anger continues to boil inside me.

"Pack a bag."

"What?" She looks up at me again, confusion lacing her delicate features. Her eyes are wide with worry.

"You can't stay here."

"I know," she says softly. "I need to book a hotel room. Or maybe I can ask Georgia if I can stay with her . . ."

"Pack a bag," I repeat slowly. "We'll figure it out once I get you out of here." I offer Ana a hand and she accepts, lowering herself carefully from the counter. "Put some shoes on, okay?"

She nods. Limping, she disappears down the hall, and I'm finally able to take a deep breath to get my need to hunt down Kress under control.

I consider sweeping the kitchen floor, then decide against it. It's his mess—let him clean it up, see his girlfriend's blood on the floor.

Part of me almost hopes Kress comes home,

because I would love to exchange some words with him right now. But I know it's better for Ana's sake if he doesn't. She doesn't need to experience any more trauma today, and she certainly doesn't need to watch me beat the shit out of him.

Ana returns, still wearing a pair of fitted jeans that show off how slender she is, and the T-shirt she had on before. But now she's in sneakers and an oversized green cardigan with the sleeves pushed up to her elbows. She's carrying a small white fluffy dog, and has a duffel bag slung over one slim shoulder.

Crossing the room toward her, I take the duffel bag and glance at the dog. "Who's this?"

She clears her throat, looking shy for a moment. "This is Hobbes."

I frown down at the creature currently wiggling in her arms. "Where can I take you?"

"I have a car," Ana says, shifting Hobbes in her arms. Clearly, the dog wants down, but with the glass still on the floor, she won't let him out of her grasp.

"Your foot isn't in great shape. Let me drive you somewhere for the night, and I'll bring you back tomorrow to get your car."

"I don't know." She chews on her lower lip, thinking it over. "Let me try my friend Georgia again."

Pulling her cell phone from her back pocket, Ana dials, listening quietly as the phone rings. The frown that pulls on her lips tells me there was no answer.

"She didn't pick up," I say.

Ana shakes her head.

"Where can I take you?"

"A hotel will be fine." Her voice is steady, even if I can tell she's a little more shaken than she's letting on.

I'm fine being the one to drive the getaway car, but she's going to need someone to lean on, someone she can talk to. And let's be honest, I'm not that guy. I need Ana's friend to pick up the phone just as much as she does.

"Which one?" I say on an exhale.

She considers it for a moment. "That place with the orange roof next to the highway should be okay."

I nod. I know of the place, but I've never stayed

there. It's a budget motel, cheap and no frills. "Got everything you need?"

"For now," she says, taking one last look around the apartment.

I hope Jason's not the vindictive type to destroy or dispose of her belongings. I doubt all the books lining those shelves are his. And it seems highly unlikely he would have picked out that funky purple armchair. But for now, I just want to get her out of here, so we have little choice but to leave it all behind.

"Is there food for him?" I ask, pausing by the door to look down at a still struggling Hobbes.

"Oh, crap. Yes, there is," Ana says, turning back toward the kitchen.

"I'll get it. Just tell me where to find it."

"In the pantry. On the floor to the left," she says, offering me a grateful smile.

I grab the small bag of dog food and then follow down the stairs behind Ana. She's not limping, which is a good sign. Maybe her foot is okay. That, or she's really good at faking.

When we reach the street, I do a quick sweep, looking for Jason, and Ana does too. Then she meets my eyes, and her mouth lifts in a shaky smile. I really have no idea how she's so composed. Maybe she's tougher than she looks, or maybe she's barely holding on and will crash into a heap when she's left to her own thoughts.

Shit.

Guiding her toward my car, I pop the trunk and place the duffel bag and dog food inside while Ana climbs in.

When I slip in beside her and start the engine, she lets out an exasperated sound.

"No, Hobbes. I have to hold you. You'll mess up the leather." Then she shoots me an apologetic look. "I'm so sorry about him. I'm sure you've never had a dog in your car. But I'll hold him the whole time, and he really doesn't shed much."

The truth is I don't even like this car. It was a stupid impulse buy after my financial advisor got on my case about the fact that I never spend any money on myself. Frankly, it pissed me off that he even noticed. But I guess when you manage other players who are buying themselves and their significant others sports cars and second homes, and vacationing in exotic locales multiple times a year, it doesn't take a theoretical physicist to string together that I wasn't exactly living large despite my $8 million salary.

My weekly visits to the grocery store and gas station, and getting my hair cut once a month, aren't exactly on par with someone pulling in millions. Even if I do shop at the fancy organic grocery store.

"Don't worry about the car. I'll have it cleaned."

She nods, still struggling to get the ten-pound beast settled in her lap.

When we reach the hotel, Ana heads inside to see if they have availability while I open the trunk to retrieve her things. But a few seconds later, she returns, shaking her head and wearing a frown.

"No vacancy?" I ask.

"The hotel doesn't allow dogs." A slow exhale leaves her lips, and her tone is defeated. "Nothing is going right for me today."

A strange knot of pressure builds inside my chest as I close the trunk again. She looks so small, so sad, standing in the parking lot holding her dog. I thought I'd outgrown emotional responses like this, but maybe the occasional pang of concern is normal. Either that or I'm going soft.

That couldn't be it, though. Protecting others has always been part of who I am. Growing up in foster care, I looked out for those smaller than me, which was most kids, since I've always been tall for my age. In hockey, I defend the puck. As the captain, I look out for my team.

And now that a woman has reached out to me and needs my help? Of course I'm going to offer it up. It's not even a question, and I don't hesitate for a second.

"Come on. Get in."

Ana climbs in beside me, dialing her friend again. There's still no answer, and she hangs up after a few minutes.

"Why don't you come to my place?" I ask. "At least to have some dinner, and you can try your friend again after we eat. Have you already eaten?"

She shakes her head and puts away her cell phone.

"Let's have something to eat, and maybe your friend will answer by then."

"Okay," she says slowly, her voice shaky. "As long as I'm not interrupting any plans you've got."

"No plans tonight."

We reach my place ten minutes later and park beneath the building in my designated parking spot. Ana waits in a strip of grass for Hobbes to pee while I unload the bags. Inside the elevator, I hit the button for the penthouse while Ana stands quietly beside me.

When I unlock the door, Hobbes goes charging inside like he owns the place while Ana flits nervously after him.

"He's fine," I say, watching him sniff the blue wool rug beneath my living room couch. "Let him explore."

"If you say so." Her eyes scan every inch of my place. "This condo is incredible."

"Thanks," I mumble.

"Have you lived here long?"

I nod. "I moved in about three years ago."

The building was new, and I put down a deposit that made my stomach cramp at the time. The condo cost $3 million, which seems crazy given that it's only two bedrooms, two bathrooms, and about 2,000 square feet. But this part of the city is pricey because it's centrally located, and I felt at ease in the minimalistic style of the finishes—light wood and quartz countertops, and large windows overlooking the city beyond.

My real estate agent even talked me into hiring an interior designer to furnish the place, which I agreed to only because I travel so much and didn't want to be bothered with picking out couches or throw pillows. It cost me a pretty penny, but when I saw the final result, I didn't regret it for a second. Decorated in shades of slate gray, blues, and creams, the effect is calming and relaxed. And exactly what I needed.

When I realize Ana's watching me, still standing silently beside the kitchen, I say, "I'll show you around if you want."

She gives me a genuine smile for the first time today. "I'd love a tour."

I show her around. The living room and kitchen are open, and there's a compact terrace beyond with two oversized rattan chairs.

"The view is amazing."

I nod. "It's nice at night. If you don't mind the sound of traffic."

She gazes out at the highway in the distance. "It doesn't bother me. I actually kind of like the sound of it. My grandparents' house was right next to a busy main road, and I'd stay there a lot in the summer. The sound of traffic kept me company as I fell asleep."

The sound of traffic reminds me of my childhood too, but I don't mention that since I don't often speak about my upbringing. Not even my teammates know I was raised in foster care before being adopted.

Inside, I head down the hallway and show her the home office, which holds a desk and my laptop, and then the master bedroom and attached bathroom.

"Oh, wow." She peeks into the huge bathroom with marble and glass and two floating vanities in sleek bamboo wood. There's a glass wall surrounding the shower, and the oversized free-standing egg-shaped bathtub takes up the far end of the room. "This is incredible."

"Thanks," I mutter, feeling self-conscious about the dirty towel on the floor and the overflowing hamper in the corner. I'm really not used to having a woman here, or a dog underfoot.

As we head back toward the kitchen, Ana pauses. "Is there a bathroom I can use?"

I tip my chin toward the hallway. "Of course. The guest bath and bedroom are right down there."

"Thanks," she murmurs, heading off.

When Ana reappears from the hall—swallowed up by that oversized cardigan, her dog at her feet, her golden hair hanging loose over her shoulders—a pang of worry hits me again. She's just so small, so damn vulnerable.

I meant what I said about helping her, even if it is a little awkward having her in my space. She didn't deserve what happened to her today. No one does. Feeling awkward, I don't know what to do with myself, shifting from foot to foot at the edge of my kitchen, muttering one-word answers.

"So, dinner." She pushes up her sleeves again. "What can I help with? I love to cook. Unless you were planning on ordering in, in which case, I'm not picky and I'll chip in."

I shake my head. "I've got it covered." Pulling open the massive fridge, I survey its contents and find eggs, milk, butter, a package of spinach that's on its last days, and a block of pepper jack cheese. "How about omelets?"

She nods, smiling. "Omelets sound great."

While I whip up the ingredients and pour the mixture into a hot skillet, Ana sits on a stool at my kitchen counter and watches me.

We eat, making small talk. It's not a skill I usually possess, but I make do, asking about where she's from—Las Vegas—and how long she's lived here—one year.

During dinner, her phone rings several times, but I assume it's not her friend, because she huffs out a sigh and eventually places the thing on silent. *Fucking Kress.*

After we eat, I make her sit on the couch while I load the dishwasher, and she does, right after pouring some dog food into a cereal bowl that she places on the floor for Hobbes. It doesn't smell very appetizing to me, but he inhales it in about twenty seconds flat.

"How's your foot?" I ask, joining her in the living room.

She slips off her sock, shrugging. "It feels all right at the moment."

"Let me see it again. If it needs it, I'll change the dressing."

"Okay," she says, nodding.

I head to the bathroom to wash my hands and gather up more gauze and tape. When I return, Ana is waiting for me with Hobbes asleep in her lap. I remove her sock, relieved to see the cut doesn't look too bad.

"How'd you get so good at this?" she asks, watching me work quickly and efficiently.

I shrug. "Hockey's a rough sport. You learn how to fix up injuries pretty quickly." I recall one of my coaches teaching me how to wrap a sprained wrist, and another showing me how to stop a nosebleed—with a tampon, of all things. I've picked up all kinds of things over the years.

Ana pushes her hair over her shoulder, and I notice a purple bruise on her wrist. I touch her forearm and gently wrap my fingers around her wrist, holding it up.

"He do this to you as well?"

She pulls it away and drops her gaze to the space between her feet.

My voice drops. "Ana?"

"He doesn't mean to, and he's never normally this rough. Things just got really heated."

My protective instincts kick into overdrive,

and I feel like breaking something. Rising to my feet without a word, I storm away, needing to cool down. Inside my bathroom, I toss the roll of athletic tape and gauze inside a drawer, barely resisting the urge to slam it shut.

I take a couple of deep breaths to get myself under control, and when I'm calmer, I march back into the living room where Ana is still waiting. She looks up at me with a mix of worry and confusion.

Adrenaline at having discovered those bruises is still coursing hotly through me, and my posture is stiff. Hearing that this isn't a first-time thing pisses me off, and it's then that I make a decision that I hope she agrees with.

"You're not going back there. Not ever."

"I know," she says quietly. Almost like she needs to do something with her hands, she dials her friend again. There's still no answer.

"You'll stay the night here," I say. "I've got a guest room, and it's yours. It's either that, or you and I are calling every goddamn hotel in Seattle to find one for you and your dog. It's your choice, though, Ana. Are you two staying here, or are we getting on our phones and calling hotels?"

She nods, and I barely hear her when she

speaks. "I'd like to stay here for the night."

I stand from the couch with a nod. "Okay, let's get your room set up."

I grab a set of sheets and a couple of pillows from the hall closet, and Ana follows me to the guest room, which is just down the hall from my bedroom. After shaking out the sheet, I'm fitting it over the mattress when Ana touches my arm.

"I can handle it. You've done enough. Picking me up, making dinner, letting me stay here . . ."

I shake my head. "I've got it."

"Then I'll just take Hobbes out. He needs to go outside before we go to bed."

Abandoning the bed, I turn to her. "I'll take him out. You should stay off that foot."

She lifts one eyebrow. "Are you sure?"

"Positive. And I'll finish setting up the bed when I get back, so don't get any ideas while I'm gone."

"Okay, I'll leave the bed making to you, but you'll need this for when you take Hobbes outside." She hands me a tiny black plastic bag from inside her purse.

"What's this?" I ask, looking down at it.

"For his business."

Oh. Right. My eyebrows dart up. I'm going to have to pick up her dog's shit in this bag.

"Never mind, Grant. I'll take him." Ana looks almost amused by my reaction.

"I can handle it," I say gruffly.

It turns out it's not as bad of a job as I imagined since his shit is the size of a Tootsie roll.

When I get back with Hobbes, Ana has finished making up the bed, and is pulling some clothing out of her duffel bag to set on top of the dresser.

"Thought I was going to make the bed?" I ask, slightly amused.

"Oh, uh, sorry. I just wanted to help. I'm sorry. I shouldn't have done it." She drops her attention to the floor as her shoulders droop.

Fuck, what did Kress do to her?

"Hey, Ana, it's okay. Honestly, it's totally fine. You never have to say you're sorry to me, okay? And please never feel like you have to look down around me. You wanna make the bed, make it. You wanna cook, cook. You wanna watch a chick flick, watch one."

Her eyes meet mine and a thankful smile lifts her lips. "Okay, Grant. Thank you."

"Will you be okay in here?" I ask, rubbing one hand over the back of my neck. I realize that I've never had someone stay in my guest room before. It's a little surreal seeing her stack of clean clothes for tomorrow and a floral-patterned toiletry bag on the dresser.

"Yes, it's perfect. Thank you for everything. I truly mean that."

With nothing more to do, I don't want to linger, so I grunt an affirmative and head to my room. On the way, I lock the front door and turn off the lights in the apartment, still trying to wrap my head around the events of today that led to a woman sleeping just down the hall from me. It certainly wasn't what I expected when I woke up this morning.

Inside my room, I strip off my jeans and T-shirt, tossing them onto the overflowing hamper, and vow to myself to take care of it tomorrow. I'm wearing black boxer briefs, my usual sleeping attire, and trying to decide if I need to put something more on, when Hobbes comes barreling in and launches himself onto my bed.

Ana is right behind him, her eyes widening as she takes me in. Pausing at the partially open door, she makes a choking sound as her gaze tracks down my chest and over my abs, then lower to the bulge inside my briefs. Her chest shutters as she releases a breath, and her face turns pink.

When I clear my throat, she stammers out an apology and darts away, only to return a second later with another apology but doesn't look my way. This time, she grabs Hobbes from my bed, where he's busy wagging his tail, and disappears down the hall with him tucked under her arm.

Chuckling softly, I close my door, making sure it's latched this time, and climb into bed. It's been a long day that started with practice, so when my head hits the pillow, I don't expect to feel so unsettled.

Even though I should be tired, I don't know how I'll get to sleep. All I want to do is hunt Kress down and kick his ass for putting fear in Ana, for leaving those bruises on her skin and scars on her soul.

CHAPTER FOUR

Moving On

Ana

The brisk air nips at my already rosy cheeks as I shuffle down the street, Hobbes scampering ahead of me. I swear, if I ever took this little rascal off the leash during a walk, I'd never see him again.

I imagine Grant taking Hobbes out, like he did last night, his giant shadow paired with the pup's tiny one. I smile, a little sadly, as I watch Hobbes sniff the new sidewalk, grass, and mailboxes. It must be a thrill to experience a new place. I wish I felt the same way.

Grant's neighborhood is absolutely stunning, with ornate buildings and even a little park around the corner. I don't spend too much time admiring my surroundings, however, because I know I won't be here for long. My thoughts are stuck in a slow spin, focusing on *why* I'm here in Grant's neighborhood instead of my own, and where I'll end up after I leave Grant's later today. Georgia's, most likely.

I yawn, even though I slept like a baby.

Grant's guest room has some really nice features, most notably the queen-size, memory-foam bed that lulled me into a deep slumber last night. I dreamed about the previous evening, but none of the damage and heartbreak. Instead, I dreamed about Grant's hands on my foot, wrapping my cuts with a touch softer than I would have imagined from a man of his size. I only woke up because Hobbes was tearing around the room, desperate to go pee.

Since I woke up before Grant, I have the upper hand. It may be strange to some to think of interactions in such a strategic way, but when you've lived with a volatile partner for as long as I have, it becomes second nature. Getting up early means I can wear out the little guy with a walk, which means he'll be less likely to cause a ruckus in the condo and potentially annoy Grant. I can also take care of coffee and breakfast when I get back, as a gesture of gratitude to this virtual stranger who has been so unbelievably kind to me.

What's in it for him?

I have to gently remind myself that some people just do good things, regardless of reciprocity. With my mind on breakfast and my stomach grumbling, I coax Hobbes back in the direction of Grant's condo. He was thoughtful enough to lend me a spare key.

Yesterday was so unexpected. *Grant* was unexpected. The way his lips pressed into a firm, straight line as he studied the cuts on my foot. The careful way he stepped in to help me.

I watched, helpless, as his jaw clenched and unclenched. It was obvious he was thinking about saying something. What, I had no idea, because apparently Grant is a man of few words. But that's okay because I'm an expert at reading between the lines, and it was obvious he was pissed off about something.

On the elevator trip up to his floor, I contemplate my next move. I'll have to get ahold of Georgia.

Once we're inside, I give Hobbes his breakfast, oddly satisfied by the familiar crunching of kibble. The bathroom door is closed, a dim light peeking from the crevice just above the floor. Steam seeps out. Grant must be in the shower.

I'm suddenly struck with an image of him, all lathered up with soap, water streaming in curving torrents down his defined muscles.

My stomach flips and I blink my eyes hard, knocking that vision right out of my head. It certainly doesn't help that I have a very good idea of what Grant's naked body looks like. *Since I barged into his room like a perverted lunatic last night . . . a real class act, Ana.*

He's a large man, several inches taller than Jason, and broad, well, everywhere. You'd have to be blind not to notice how attractive he is, but I force the thoughts from my head.

Bread, eggs, brown sugar, butter, maple syrup . . . Grant has all the ingredients for French toast, I realize with a grin. I wasn't lying when I told him that I love to cook. I'm not particularly adventurous with my kitchen experiments, and I'll admit that they don't always turn out like I hope. But the classics I have down to a science.

I crack the eggs and get to work, enjoying the sizzle of butter in the pan. Coffee trickles into the pot, percolating quickly in Grant's fancy, expensive-looking coffee machine. The bread he has is fresh, like bakery bread, as if he just picked it up yesterday. I'm so engrossed with my work that I don't notice the bathroom door opening down the hall, or the footsteps drawing near.

"Good morning."

I jump with a gasp, dropping the spatula on the floor with a clatter. Grant steps forward, one hand raised in apology. Feeling silly for being so jumpy, I reach to pick up a dish towel. There's some gunk on the hardwood floor, and I wipe it up.

"Sorry."

"No, I'm sorry for scaring you. People say I'm quiet on my feet for such a big guy," Grant says, reaching down to pick up the spatula before I have the chance.

I get a nice long look at his muscular arms, testing the seams of his T-shirt sleeves. My breath escapes my chest in a whoosh.

"You are a big guy, yeah." I laugh, and then immediately correct myself. "Broad, tall, muscular." *Why am I describing him to himself? Breathe.*

Grant doesn't seem to notice my awkward fumbling. Instead, he carries the spatula to the sink and rinses it off before bringing it back to me. "What are you making?"

"French toast."

"I haven't had French toast in years. It smells good." He focuses on the pan on the stove before turning back to me. "Did you sleep okay?"

"Yes," I say, my anxiety slowly melting away like butter in the pan. "Hobbes too."

"Good to hear," Grant says with a grunt as the coffeemaker beeps. "Mind if I turn on the TV?"

"Nope, all good. I'll finish making breakfast."

Grant pours two cups of coffee, then slides one across the counter to me. He doesn't bother telling me where the cream and sugar live, since I've already acquainted myself with his kitchen. He steps into the living room, his bare feet leaving imprints in the blue wool carpet that spills out from underneath his couch. *I really like that carpet.*

As Grant flips through the channels, voices carry into the kitchen. Commercials, news reports, entertaining morning shows. For some reason, it reminds me of when I used to cook dinner for Dad while he watched the Monday night football game. My heart swells at the unexpected memory, and

I'm suddenly positive this will be the best French toast I've ever made.

When I carry two plates to the living room, I find Grant on his feet, the remote suspended in his hand. He stares at the screen, his mouth pulled into a grim line. I follow his gaze to see one of those entertainment newscasts.

"We're back from our break," a male journalist says in a deep, smooth voice. "And just like we promised, we have breaking news on everyone's favorite hockey team."

Suddenly, Jason's face is on the screen. My chest seizes painfully as I hold my breath.

"Jason Kress, left winger for the Seattle Ice Hawks, was caught on film this week in a physical altercation with a woman he's reported to have been in a relationship with for two years. Please be warned the footage you are about to see may cause distress to viewers, so please turn away if needed."

The screen changes to black-and-white security footage. I recognize it as the hotel hallway adjacent to the spa where I work.

There's no audio, but a large man yells at a small woman before taking her roughly by the arm and yanking her down the hall at a pace she can barely keep up with. While they wait for the elevator, she speaks to him, placing a timid hand on his shoulder. The doors slide open and he forcibly shoves her inside, where she crumples to the floor like a rag doll, broken, fearful, and crying. He steps inside, and as the doors slide shut, the woman and the monster hovering over her disappear.

I watch the entire exchange as though it happened to someone else.

The journalist is back now, but I can only make out a few words and phrases like *abusive*, *domestic violence*, *physical*, and something about *potential suspension*. The announcer's voice sounds garbled, like I'm floating in deep water.

When I realize I haven't breathed for nearly half a minute, I pull in a deep, shaky breath, but my gaze remains locked on the photo of Jason that now fills the television screen.

"Ana, look at me. Let's sit down."

Recognizing Grant's steady hand on my shoulder, I nod and sit on his couch, never letting my eyes leave the screen. They play the footage again, this time in slow motion, and I'm instantly thrown back to that moment. I was scared of the look in Jason's eyes, scared of how far he'd go. Then the screen goes black.

I blink and turn to look at Grant, who gently sets the remote on the coffee table. He's looking at me, concern drawn with heavy lines into his expression.

"We don't need to watch that again." His jaw is tense and his face is unreadable, aside from those dark brows that are pulled together in concentration.

I wish I knew what he was thinking. Wish I knew what it means when his full lips press together in a solemn line. Wish he never had to see that.

"Okay," I whisper, clutching my hands together in my lap to stop them from fidgeting.

"When did that happen?"

"A couple weeks ago, I think." My voice comes out hoarse. I'd completely forgotten that it happened. *I've been in survival mode for so long . . . I must have wiped it away. So much easier that way.*

Grant's phone starts ringing from the kitchen, but he ignores it. And then I hear my own phone, back in the bedroom, buzzing with text notifications too. I ignore it as well.

"So I'm supposed to believe he really isn't

'normally rough' with you?"

I bristle at the question and don't respond. Grant's tone isn't harsh, but his words do sting. He looks like he has more questions. But rather than ask them, he clenches his jaw, locking his words away, and I'm grateful. *I don't know how much more humiliation I can take in one sitting.*

His eyes are deep, soulful. They might even be pretty if it weren't for the look of flat resignation reflecting back at me from their depths. The most infuriating thing about him, though, is that he seems to lack all basic human emotion. I'd rather he yell at me, *scream*, admit he thinks I'm an idiot for staying with Jason—anything but that deep, haunted look he's giving me.

I told him at my apartment that Jason isn't normally rough with me—and he's not. But sometimes, well, sometimes he is, and those situations have the potential to get really bad. But he always stops himself before things get out of hand. That's the truth.

But I can see, based on Grant's expression, that's not good enough. I can also tell that Grant's the kind of man who would never lose his temper and turn violent.

Unable to take his silence any longer, I swallow and sigh. "I think I'm going to call my friend again," I murmur.

His expression is dark and brooding, and he says nothing.

Rising to my feet, I wander like a ghost back to the guest room.

My phone has been plugged into its charger, and now it lights up with missed call notifications. *Jason. Jason. Jason. Georgia. Jason. Georgia. Elise. Becca. Jason.*

I stare at the phone, my fingers numb against the smooth screen. It lights up again, and my heart skips a beat. *Georgia.*

"Hello?"

"Oh my God, Ana! Are you okay?"

"I'm okay," I hear myself say, not sure if that's entirely the truth. I quickly realize it's my go-to response these days.

"I'm so, so sorry I missed your calls. I took one of those sleeping pills, *early*, at like eight last night, because I'm a practically a grandma and— Oh my God, you don't need to hear this! I need to hear about you! Where are you right now?"

"I'm okay," I say again, this time more confidently. Georgia's chattering somehow draws me back from that cold, underwater place. I'm thinking a little more clearly now. "I'm with a friend."

"Okay, good, because Jason is looking for you. He came to my apartment!"

"What?" *Oh God.*

"Yeah, he was banging on my door at like five o'clock this morning. Screaming your name. Definitely drunk. I guess he thought you were with me. I didn't answer, I was so terrified!"

"I'm so sorry, Georgie . . ."

"Shut up, don't apologize! You're not the crazy one. This is his fault. Anyway, I've been calling you since he left. I just needed to know that you're good."

"I'm good, I promise. Thank you for checking on me."

The line goes quiet for a moment, and then she asks, "Have you seen the news?"

I grimace, closing my eyes. "Yes."

"Honey, the tape looked like that hallway at work. I had no idea he did that to you. I was just in the other room. I could have . . ." She pauses, not equipped with the right words for situations like these. Neither am I.

"No, Georgie, it's no one's fault. I didn't tell anyone, so there's nothing that could have been done." Those words are a lie. *It's my fault.* Tears unexpectedly well in my eyes. With a deep breath, I try to calm myself.

"Okay . . . but I'm not sure if I agree with you on that one. I *want* to help. How can I help?"

"Well, I really don't think I should go into work today. I don't know if Jason will be there waiting for me, or if he'll show up later. Although I'll probably have to talk to him at some point—"

"No way. You're not coming in today. As badly as I want to see you and hug you, you're taking the day off. Actually, take off as much time as you need."

I smile. Sometimes I really do appreciate her pushiness. And it also helps that she's my manager. "Thanks, G."

"Don't worry. I've got your back."

Georgia agrees to cover for me today, and my relief is instantaneous. We hang up with promises to talk later tonight. Even though I'd intended to ask Georgia if I could stay with her, the fact that Jason visited her apartment has me shaken, and I chickened out.

My phone still has twenty-one missed calls on it . . . seventeen of which are from Jason. My thumb hovers over the CALL BACK button.

Somewhere else in the apartment, a phone rings.

"Hello?" Grant's voice comes from the other room as he answers the call.

I set down my cell phone on the duvet and tread carefully back to the living room. When I enter the room again, Grant is pacing back and forth, one hand clenched tightly around his cell phone and the other shoved deep in the pocket of his jeans.

"Yeah. I became involved yesterday."

I strain to hear the other side of the conversation, but it's just a low buzz. *Who is he talking to?*

"She's somewhere safe."

A little ball of tension in my chest unravels. Grant didn't tell this mystery person where I am . . . that I'm staying at his condo. And I appreciate that more than he probably realizes.

"She's a fighter. She has bruises, sir."

Sir?

Grant's gaze locks with mine, and softens for a moment. I don't have enough time to read it before he turns away again. A lump sits heavy in my throat, threatening to choke me with emotion.

Am I really a fighter? Or am I just a survivor?

"I think that's for the best. Thanks for the heads-up," Grant says, his voice gruff. He exchanges good-byes and hangs up, shoving his phone deep into his back pocket.

"That was Coach," he says, answering my un-asked question.

"Oh." I let out a relieved breath. "What did he say?"

"They were working out a trade to New England for Kress—for your—for Jason," Grant says, seemingly trying to pick the least damaging words to say. "I'm not sure if you knew that."

I shake my head. Jason never said anything.

"But with this morning's news, that's fallen through. And now they're talking about suspension."

My eyebrows shoot up. "Really?"

He nods gravely. "The league takes this kind of thing very seriously."

A pregnant pause hovers between us, except for the scuffling of my dog's feet on the tile floor of the kitchen. Poor Hobbes has no idea what's going on, and he's as cheerful as ever.

I pick up our uneaten plates of French toast and take them back to the kitchen, setting them neatly on the counter before I pick up Hobbes and carry him to the guest room with me. Grant follows, leaning against the door frame with one arm above his head.

"What are you doing?" he asks when I begin stuffing what little I brought with me back into my suitcase, and Hobbes circles my feet anxiously.

"I'm leaving. Thank you so much for your hospitality, but I should really pack up and move to my friend Georgia's place for now."

It's the only thing I can do. I don't want to complicate things for Grant. He's been so nice to me. Maybe there's a reason why he couldn't tell his coach where I am. Maybe me being here will cause a problem for him. I can't have that.

"Are you going to go to work today?" he asks, his voice disapproving.

"Maybe." I shrug, feigning a casual posture in the midst of all the craziness I've landed in.

"You can't," he says, his voice low and firm. "Jason knows where you work. Does he know where your friend lives?"

I sigh. Grant's right. I just don't want to admit it.

"Yeah, he does. He went there this morning." My hands pause on the zipper when I hear Grant move into the room. With one step toward me, the whole room seems to shift, suddenly growing so much smaller.

"Don't you think he'll try again? He knows where to look for you. I don't want to scare you, but he's going to be volatile even more so now that the video has been broadcast. And when he gets word of the suspension, he'll be a ticking bomb."

I chew on my lip.

"I don't want you to get hurt, Ana, and I don't want him getting anywhere near you. I think it's best if you stay here."

I meet Grant's eyes, and for once, he doesn't

look away from me immediately. Instead, he holds my gaze, and I hold his.

As much as I'd like to pretend I've got all of this under control, I really don't. I am that rag doll of a woman on the television screen, propped up by only a fragile self-esteem and a faltering sense of direction.

"Okay." My voice comes out as a hushed whisper.

Grant lets go of a breath he's been holding.

Oh my God, he's relieved. Grant is relieved that I'm staying with him. He wants to protect me. These thoughts barrel through the noise banging around in my head, clear and resonant among the rest.

"Good," he says with a grunt. "Should we eat first, or do you want to go and get your car?"

I remember the now-cold breakfast I'd been so excited about. Now with my stomach still tied in a knot, I doubt I could eat a bite. "Let's just get it over with and get my car."

He nods. "You got it. Come on."

Grant leaves the room, but an outline of his shape in the doorway remains, imprinted on my eyes. The world suddenly feels larger again, unfamiliar and wild, but also safer than it has in days.

I pick up my purse and shove my phone in it, then follow him to the front door, where he's putting on his coat. He holds out my cardigan, and arm by arm, I slip into its warmth. I meet his eyes, giving him a genuine smile for the first time today.

He nods back. Apparently, a smile isn't quite in his emotional vocabulary.

I chuckle. For a moment, I almost forget the context of this situation. *Isn't that odd?* The closer I stand to Grant, the safer I feel. Still, he isn't quite a white knight from the storybooks my mom used to read to me.

But that doesn't change the fact that I'm in need of a little rescuing right now.

CHAPTER FIVE
Emotional Battlefield

Ana

When Grant dropped me off at my car, he insisted on waiting with me until I was tucked safely inside, despite the fact that Jason's car was nowhere to be seen. He asked me what I was going to do with the rest of my day, and I assured him I would be perfectly fine. After a little convincing, he let me pull out of the parking lot of my building, then followed me out, his car trailing closely behind mine for the first mile or two until he turned away toward the training facility.

It's strange to think that Jason and Grant will be skating across the same ice today . . . especially after the look in Grant's eyes when he saw the bruise on my arm.

I'm crossing my fingers that nothing dramatic

happens at practice today. *That's the last thing I need right now. More drama.*

I waved confidently to Grant as he drove away. But now, sitting behind the steering wheel of my ten-year-old Nissan Altima, I really don't know what to do with myself. I told Georgia I wouldn't go to work, but it's a quarter to nine, the start of my workday, and I still have plenty of time to get there. My anxiety is getting the better of me with every passing minute.

Truth be told, I really need to do something with my hands today. Plus, now I'm faced with the very real scenario in which I have to move out and begin paying rent, solely on my less-than-ideal salary. Jason and I had worked out a fair enough payment plan where each of us paid a certain pro-portion of our salaries . . . well, before he started gambling. Then everything went off the rails.

Jason.

Will he come to the spa? He's done it before, as the whole hockey-following world now knows. By now he's probably at the training facility . . . and no doubt he's seen the news report. *He wouldn't risk it, right?* Jason may be a lot of things, but he's not an idiot.

By the time I pull into the hotel parking lot, I've convinced myself. Jason won't come to my place of work unless he plans to leave in handcuffs, not to mention that he'll most certainly get kicked off the team for walking out of practice. He cares about his hockey career too much to do something like that.

The look on Georgia's face when I walk through the front door is one of pure shock. She mouths to me, *What are you doing here?* I only smile back and give her a weak thumbs-up. She shakes her head at me, clearly appalled at my choice to put myself out here in the open like this.

I want to assure her that everything is okay, but we've already welcomed our morning appointments. That doesn't stop Georgia from sneaking a glance at me every so often. *Probably looking for bruises.*

But the day crawls by, just like any other. Jason never makes an appearance, no drama ensues, and the world keeps spinning. By the end of our shifts, Georgia and I are smiling and laughing, as if today were just a normal day. As if Jason had never stepped into my life.

An alarm on my phone reminds me that I'll need to take out Hobbes soon, or he'll definitely ruin that beautiful wool rug in Grant's living room. Since Georgia took my last appointment of the day, I have just enough time after work to pick up some groceries.

Grant's kitchen is gorgeous and much more modern than mine, but there isn't a lot of food. Everything in his fridge seems strictly devoted to protein fueling and meal prepping, understandable for an athlete on a strict schedule. I'm already inconveniencing him enough; I don't want to mess with that.

At the store, I pick out the essentials for my favorite meals, gathering the ingredients for lasagna, pork chops, stir fry, tacos, and meatloaf. In the produce aisle, I hold my phone limply, debating whether to text Grant and ask if he has any food allergies. I decide against it, remembering how annoyed Jason would get if I texted him while he was busy at practice.

But Grant isn't Jason, is he? Grant is kind, and thoughtful, and reserved . . .

I find myself smiling, somehow knowing that, regardless of what I buy today, Grant will take it in stride. At least I know he's not vegetarian or vegan. Those omelets he made were freaking fantastic. My mouth waters at the thought, and I hear my mother's voice in the back of my mind, chirping, *Don't shop on an empty stomach, Ana! You'll walk away with the whole store.* I look down at my cart load of groceries and frown. *Whoops.*

Once everything is paid for, I load the groceries into the trunk of my car and take the freeway back to Grant's condo. Before long, I'm struggling to open his front door, two paper bags full of food threatening to spill onto the nice, carpeted floor of the hall. The door swings open and I gasp, nearly losing my balance and toppling across the threshold. Grant steadies me with his strong hands on my shoulders.

"Hey," he says, giving me with a perplexed look. Hobbes jumps up, putting his little paws against my knees with a cheerful yip. Grant reaches for the grocery bags before I can object.

"Hi! Oh, thank you." I let Grant take both bags from me, suddenly empty-handed in his threshold. Kicking off my boots, I shake my head with a small smile creeping across my lips. Will I ever get used to this level of chivalry? *Doubtful.*

"This is a lot of food," he says matter-of-factly as we trek toward the kitchen, Hobbes close on our heels.

I begin unpacking the cold foods, pulling out the produce and frozen meats first. "It's the least I can do. If it's all right with you, I'd like to make the meals while I'm staying here, as a thank-you for letting me stay. For everything." *Why does my voice sound so high-pitched?*

As I lean into the fridge, making room for the new groceries, Grant seems to mull over my offer for a moment. *Too bad. I've already made up my mind, mister!*

Then I wonder if he's right. Maybe this *is* too much food, and buying it implies that I plan to mooch off of him for longer than he anticipated. I feel my resolve slip, ever so slightly.

"It's not that much," I say weakly. "We'll get through it quickly. And you can keep whatever we don't get to when I find somewhere else to stay."

Grant's eyes flash, and my breath catches. I can't tell what he's thinking, and I take a deep breath.

"I'm sure we'll get through it all. I have a good appetite," he says with a nod, then leaves the kitchen and heads down the hall.

Suddenly, I'm annoyed. Would it kill this man to crack a smile? I decide that's the goal for tonight. I will make Grant smile with whatever food I whip up for the two of us. Right after I—

"I already took the dog out," Grant calls from the bathroom. "You can take your coat off."

I frown, looking down at Hobbes. He wags his tail, happy to have my attention, blissfully unaware of the upheaval our lives have been thrown into.

"Thank you!" I call back. I chuckle to myself, watching Hobbes roll around on the hardwood floors like he's a puppy again. He really loves it here, the little traitor.

I hear the shower start in the bathroom and a sensation of warmth floods over me. Perspiration forming on the back of my neck, I take off my jacket and return it to the front hall closet. It's nice to have someone else walk Hobbes for once. It's been my sole responsibility for the past three years that I've had him. Lord knows Jason never volunteered. *Another point for Grant.*

With these odd but pleasant thoughts brewing, I begin dinner. Lasagna is a no-brainer; it's quick and easy and always a winner, as long as you don't overcook the noodles. I start the sauce, letting it simmer while I arrange fresh ricotta and lasagna noodles in a glass baking dish that I find in a nearby cabinet.

Once the sauce meets my standards, I finish assembling the lasagna and place into the pre-heated oven. Within minutes, the kitchen is warm and fragrant.

I've pulled my thick hair up with a heavy-duty hair tie into a loose bun on top of my head. Based on my reflection in the glass of the window, my cheeks are red, so I grab a glass of water to cool off.

My ears perk up as I finally hear the steady stream of Grant's shower halt. I can't help but be amused by the length of his shower—I've been toiling away in here for at least a half hour. I guess when you have a body like that, one so big and bulky, you need more time to wash.

And here I am again, thinking about a naked Grant. I down the rest of the water in three choking gulps.

When he reappears, wearing a T-shirt and sweatpants, I'm coughing pretty violently.

"Are you okay?" he asks, his brow furrowed in that classic look of worry he wears so well. His skin is rosier than it usually is, no doubt from the scalding water raining down on his flawless skin

. . .

"Wrong pipe," I say, wheezing as I wave away his concern. *Thank God he put some clothes on.* I definitely wouldn't have recovered if he'd come out in a towel.

"It smells great. Can I help?"

I'm struck speechless for a moment by the good-natured tone of his voice before I nod and point to the salad bowl resting near an assortment of vegetables.

"Cut the rest of the tomatoes and cucumbers?" I say when my voice returns.

As Grant gets right to work, I'm impressed with our ability to cohabitate this space as practical strangers. We dance around each other with ease, Grant moving between the sink and the counter, and me checking on the oven's contents after adding frozen garlic bread and setting plates on the dining table.

I hear the pop of a bottle of wine being uncorked, and turn to see Grant pouring two glasses of a deep red cabernet.

He's a wine drinker. Huh.

"Dinner won't be ready for another fifteen minutes," I say apologetically.

Grant shakes his head, passing one of the wineglasses to me. When he extends his arm, I notice a nearly imperceptible wince flicker across his expression.

"There's no rush," he says, his voice tight with the effort of masking pain.

"Are you okay?" I ask, my healer's instinct making me reach out involuntarily to feel his shoulder.

I quickly retract my hand, suddenly aware of a line being crossed. My impulse is always to help, and my expertise is touch, but I don't want him to feel uncomfortable by disregarding his boundaries. Luckily, Grant seems to think nothing of it, merely rotating his shoulder in small, focused circles.

"It's nothing," he says with a short sigh. "I . . . knocked my shoulder on the ice today, and it's still feeling pretty sore."

Grant doesn't seem like the type to go down easily. My twisted imagination takes me down the darkest path, imagining a certain dick-headed teammate slamming into his unsuspecting team captain in foul play.

"Okay, drink that," I say firmly, pointing to his untouched glass of wine, "and then lay down on your stomach."

"What?" Grant's eyes go wider than I've ever seen them.

"I'm going to help you loosen up, speed up the healing process," I say, my gentle voice practiced by years of massage therapy. "You'll see that I'm very good at this."

"It's really fine," he starts to object, but I'm already on my feet, gesturing for him to get into position.

He needs a massage, and I'm determined to help him in any way that I can. *After he's been so accommodating to me, a shoulder massage is no trouble at all.* I try not to think too hard about the excitement brewing low in my belly, my fingers aching to touch this man who seems to be made entirely of firm, yet supple muscle.

He gives me another uncertain look.

"Come on, we don't have much time before dinner's ready. I promise it won't take long."

Grant's expression changes to one that's half amused, half frustrated. He tosses back a significant gulp of red wine and huffs a little before laying his long, lean body across the couch cushions.

From this perspective, I have a good view of his broad shoulders, which taper into his sinewy back and down to his trim waist and muscular butt. The man is fully clothed, but something about the fit of his cotton shirt and sweatpants makes me feel like I'm spying on something entirely indecent.

It's strange that I even notice since Jason has the body of an athlete too. He's tall, five foot eleven to my five foot two. But Jason's midsection was soft—a dad bod, he liked to joke. There's nothing soft about Grant, though, and he towers over me at a solid six feet, four inches.

"Do your worst," he says grimly, his cheek squished adorably against the soft fabric of the couch.

I lean my hips against his for support, one leg curled up next to his torso on the couch and the other hanging off the edge, my toes tangled in the wool carpet. I won't straddle Grant, although that would give me a much better angle to work from . . . that would be crossing a line. With soft hands, I lightly rub his shoulder, focusing on the sore trapezius. I know how firm this guy is, but I'm still surprised when the muscle doesn't budge under my touch.

"You're very tense," I say, my voice low. I work my hands into a deeper, more meaningful press, eliciting a strangled moan from beneath me.

"Fuck, Ana . . ." Grant groans, his eyes fluttering closed.

My cheeks warm even more at the way my name sounds from his lips, his voice deep and guttural. His body remains tense beneath my fingertips, and the warmth of his skin permeates mine. My mind races with thoughts of having my hands on his body, his whole body . . .

Oh my God. What the hell is wrong with me? I need a distraction, *fast.*

"Do you have any family here, Grant?" I ask, my voice strained.

"No, not anymore."

"Why's that?"

"I grew up in Northern California with my adopted parents," he murmurs, his voice filled with something like . . . trust.

I'm pleased that he's sharing such personal information with me, because I have a strong feeling that he doesn't share information about his past with a lot of people. I didn't know he was adopted. It occurs to me that Jason definitely doesn't know either, so this isn't information Grant shares, even with his teammates.

"How old were you when you were adopted?" I ask, genuinely curious.

"Six," he says with a sigh. "You can go harder if you'd like."

I smirk. Yes, I would like.

I dig my thumbs into his shoulders, now easing both sides of his broad back into a state of deep relaxation. More than with anyone else in my whole career, I'm *loving* the feel of this giant man melting beneath my fingertips. *Maybe that's the red wine talking.*

"I don't remember much about the foster homes I was in before," he murmurs. "I was adopted by an older couple, and they raised me right. My dad was a huge hockey fan, so he signed me up for minimite camp when I was little. I worked hard at it because I wanted to make him proud. And now here I am."

I smile, charmed by the unexpected insight I now have into Grant's life. I dig the heel of my hand into a knot I can feel under his shoulder blade, and he releases another groan. Then I reluctantly give his back a little pat, letting him know that the massage has ended. After a moment, he sits back up, several inches closer to me now than he was before.

"I'm sure they're very proud of you," I say, my gaze wandering lazily over his facial features. Dark lashes . . . full lips. A chiseled jaw.

"They were, yeah." Grant's eyes are suddenly downcast.

Oh no.

"Were?" I ask carefully as I hand him his wine-glass, and his warm fingers brush against mine.

He nods and takes a sip. "They were older when they adopted me. Dad passed six years ago, and Mom followed almost three years ago."

"I'm so sorry," I murmur, my heart aching for this man who has experienced so much loss. *Just like me.* I open my mouth to tell him about the loss of my own mother, but think better of it. *Another time.* I don't want to bring the conversation back to me when I'm just starting to learn more about him.

"That's all right. It's been a while, and time

heals, or whatever it is they say," he says softly, and I swear there's almost a smile on his lips when his eyes meet mine. "Thank you, though."

"I'm sorry I don't know the timeline of it all, but did they get to see you make it to the big leagues?" I feel a little embarrassed that I don't know how long Grant has been a professional hockey player. Jason always gave me shit for not paying close attention to the league, even when I tried my best to follow a sport I know so little about.

"Don't apologize," Grant says with a chuckle.

Okay, now that is *definitely* a smile. Point one for Ana.

"Yes, they saw it all. I was drafted straight out of high school, and I've been at this for . . . shit, nearly fifteen years. Sometimes, especially around the rookies, I feel like the old man on the team at thirty-two." He shakes his head a little mournfully, and I cover my giggle with one hand.

This is the most I've ever heard Grant talk. Who would have thought? Get some wine in the man and get my hands on him, and he's suddenly an open book, a book I'm particularly interested in reading.

"Since you're being so open, old man," I say,

cocking my head to one side, "would you let me take a bubble bath in that big tub of yours sometime?"

Grant's cheekbones flush a little. "Sure," he says after clearing his throat, his eyes suddenly trained on the wall behind me. "It's yours. Never once used the thing."

"Really? Thank you!"

I'm about to lean forward and peck him on the cheek when the timer on the oven beeps, popping me out of this weird bubble of intimacy we've created. Instead, I just shoot him a sly smile before scurrying off to the kitchen to plate our food.

"Do you need any help in there?" Grant calls from the next room.

Truthfully, I might, but I'd rather take a moment to catch my breath. My reflection in the kitchen window's glass shows the extent of my red wine blush . . . now creeping onto my clavicle. *You're not on a date, Ana! Get ahold of yourself.*

"No, I'm okay! Just give me a second."

It ends up taking several seconds, but soon enough I'm armed with two full plates of piping-hot lasagna, toasted garlic bread, and garden salads. I set the plates down on the dining table and take a seat as Grant digs in. I have a mouth full of arugula when he starts the conversation again.

"Can I ask you a question?"

I nod, already anticipating that this won't be an easy one to answer. No one ever starts an easy question with a precursor like that. They just ask the question.

"Do you love him?"

I swallow. *Woof!* That *is* a hard one. I take another long gulp of red wine, buying time.

Do I try to preserve formalities? Or do I tell the truth?

Grant's eyes are locked on mine, seeking the answer I've yet to spill. I can't bear to lie when he's been so honest with me tonight, so I take a deep breath, averting my gaze to the floor.

"Honestly, I'm not sure anymore. At one time, I did. But after everything that's happened, I don't think I do now."

"So, why did you stay with him?" Grant asks, his voice equal parts irritated and polite.

"Huh-uh," I say, wagging one finger in the air.

"That's not how this works. I get the next question. Then you can ask yours."

Grant cocks an eyebrow at me, clearly on to my game. I already asked him *tons* of questions before dinner began. But he concedes with a smirk, holding up his hands in mock surrender.

"Hit me."

"All right, ten questions. You already used your first one, so mine is . . . who's your favorite guy on the team?"

His expression morphs from amusement to thoughtfulness as he takes a big bite of lasagna. He *really* thinks about it, smiles, and swallows.

"Jordie. Jordan, the rookie. That might be weird, since I've known him for the least amount of time. But that might be the reason why I like him." Grant chuckles, his laughter bubbling from somewhere deep within.

Oh man. I really, *really* like that laugh.

"Plus, he wants to learn. He's hungry to improve and takes advice well, which is nice. I like feeling useful, I guess."

Nodding, I consider this. "Would you ever consider coaching after your playing career ends? You could get more of that useful feeling, helping the younger guys learn."

His eyes meet mine. "I've thought it about it, yeah."

"Okay. Your turn." I pick up the wine bottle and replenish Grant's now empty glass.

"Why did you stay with Jason?" he asks unflinchingly.

"Wow, I was hoping you'd forget that one," I say with a little breathless laugh. "You're a real hard hitter with these questions, aren't you?"

"Is that a question?" Grant asks, leaning forward with the challenge.

My cheeks grow warmer with each passing second. He's a lot more playful than I would have guessed from our first few interactions. I guess those were under less-than-playful circumstances.

"Nope," I say, popping the "p" with my lips.

His gaze drops to my mouth for a moment. Without looking away, he asks again, "So, why did you stay with him?"

I take a moment to think it over, trying to cram two years of emotional turmoil into a simple answer. *That's just not possible.* I can only do my best to explain how I'm feeling at this very moment. I take a sharp breath, holding it for a moment before releasing it. Then I meet his eyes.

"First, I'm not with him any longer. I just need to tell him that it's over, and I plan to do that. To-night."

Grant searches my face, looking for a dent in the new armor I've recently donned. He won't find any, however, because I've made up my mind.

I'm not happy with Jason, and he's clearly not happy with me. I was afraid to leave him for so long, terrified of his reaction and daunted by the possibility of living my life alone again. But the reality is, I've been alone in this relationship for a year now. The physical abuse was only one part of a larger, more problematic codependence. And, truth be told, I'm ready to cut myself out of it.

"I'm glad to hear that," Grant finally says, his voice low and steady.

Relieved, I smile up at him. "My turn. What's your favorite color?"

"Blue. What's yours?"

"Purple. Your favorite kind of cuisine?"

"Greek. Yours?"

"Italian," I say, sheepishly nodding to the remnants of lasagna on my plate.

"Makes sense," he says with a nod. "Next question."

"What number is this?"

"Well, it was four, but with that question it's five, and it's my turn."

"Damn!" I cry, leaning into a full, belly laugh. I hold my belly, realizing I've consumed too much pasta to be laughing this hard.

"What made you get into massage therapy?" he asks, his brows raised in an open expression of curiosity.

"I studied kinesthesiology in college and fell into it pretty naturally. I used to give my parents massages, and I've always fed off that pleasure I can give people with my hands. It feels good to help people relax," I say with a shrug. "There's nothing too deep about it."

"Noted," Grant says with a nod.

My turn.

"When's the last time you went on a date?" I

ask, pointing at him with an accusatory index finger.

His eyes go comically wide for a moment before squinting with difficulty.

"Wow," I finally say. "It's taking you a long time to answer that one. Has it been that long?"

"Is that your final question?" Grant asks, and I roll my eyes, giving him a vague *get on with it* gesture. "Yes, it's been a really long time."

"Your turn." I motion for him to go ahead, pushing my plate away.

"When did your mom pass?" Grant asks, his voice suddenly solemn.

How did he . . . I stare at him blankly for a moment before responding.

"Almost fifteen years ago," I say, my voice a little tighter than usual. "She died in a car accident when I was young, late at night. I still have trouble sleeping when it storms."

Grant nods, his big hands clasped before him. "I'm sorry to pry."

"That's okay," I say, the tension in my throat dissipating. "It's only fair after I grilled you about your parents earlier. What were their names?"

"Bob and Linda," Grant says. "How about yours?"

"Loretta was my mother, and my dad is Pat. He's a big football fan. Not so much hockey."

"Ahh." Grant chuckles, shaking his head from side to side.

Suddenly, this really does feel like a date. I now know a lot more about Grant . . . probably more than his teammates do.

What did I think I was accomplishing by suggesting this game?

Shame creeps behind my heart and wraps itself around me with a tight grip. I shouldn't be having this much fun with another man when my life is in shambles . . . when I still haven't officially ended things with Jason.

"Well, we haven't quite made it to ten, but if I don't wash these plates now, I never will," I say with exaggerated pep. I stand, shaking out the leg that's nearly fallen asleep. *Pins and needles, ouch!* I wince, limping, as I pick up our empty plates.

"Let me take care of that," Grant says, taking the plates from my hands. "You made the food, so

I can do the clean-up."

Once again, I'm left empty-handed, thinking about words like *chivalry* and *sexy.* I blink, taming my grin into a small smirk. "That seems like a decent arrangement."

When he's almost out of the room, I spin, a question on my lips. "Hey, Grant?"

He turns around. "Yeah?"

"Can I ask you a question? Outside of the game." I clasp my fingers together before me, anxiously twisting them around each other.

Grant relaxes his stance, his face open and listening. "Sure," he says with a short nod.

"Any news on the suspension?"

Grant's shoulders heave and he lets out a deep sigh. "Yeah. It'll be announced in the morning." His lips part with an unasked question, and after only a moment, he gives in. "Have you talked to him yet?"

I shake my head. "I'm going to reach out tonight."

"Okay," Grant says, but his gaze shifts from mine to the plates in his hands. "Let me know if you need anything." And with that, he leaves the room.

I take a deep, uneven breath. Tonight has been all fun and games, but now it's time to remember myself. Remember my life. Remember the mess I still have to clean up, even if I wasn't the one to make it.

I walk the short distance down the hall to the guest room and close the door behind me, resting my forehead against the cool wooden surface. In the kitchen, the water is running, a loud and steady stream that Grant is no doubt using to wash our dinner dishes. I have the time and privacy to call Jason and finally end things.

But when I pick up my phone to place the call, my hands are shaking. The idea of hearing Jason's voice and the inevitable screaming match that will follow is something I don't want to live through ever again. Maybe it's immature, or even cowardly, but I'm going to text him. I need control in this situation, and I don't trust myself to keep my cool with Jason's voice in my ear.

> Jason, I don't want to hurt you, but it's important that I do this. I can't be with you anymore. Our relationship has caused me more

```
damage than good, and I need to
find the good in my life again. I
only wish you well.
```

I read the message twenty times, editing and tweaking until I'm about to lose my damn mind.

Frustrated, I flop down on the bed, sinking deep into the plush duvet. Squeezing my eyes closed, I try to imagine Jason's face when he opens this message after twenty-four hours of being ignored, and a suspension from his one true love, hockey, looming in the near future. The hurt and betrayal etched deep into his eyes . . . the tight line of his lips, holding back a curse. The hot, salty tears I've spent years wiping away.

No, Ana. He's not your responsibility any longer.

I open my eyes, lift my phone, and press SEND.

I wait for the revelatory moment, the sensation of blissful freedom, but it doesn't come. I'm officially a single woman now, but I feel exactly the same. The corners of my eyes prick with tears, even as I smile. And when my phone vibrates with a call from Jason, I turn it off, setting it onto the nightstand without so much as a second thought.

Curling into a ball, I take yet another deep

breath. I hear faint footsteps in the hall as Grant moves from the kitchen to his own bedroom. The soft padding of his socks against the hardwood floor fills me with a comfort I'm only recently beginning to recognize.

I'm safe here.

Tears slide freely down my cheeks as I laugh quietly, recounting our strange evening of conversation. Grant is stubborn and a little grumpy. He's also wealthy, handsome, and single, which is obviously none of my business. But I can tell, underneath all that gruffness, Grant really is a good guy.

And I could use some goodness in my life.

CHAPTER SIX

Second Chances

Grant

Waiting for the coffee to finish brewing, I lean one hip against the counter and scrub a hand over my face.

Last night with Ana took an unexpected turn. We had dinner and some wine, which was fine . . . until she prodded me into opening up. It's something I rarely do, even with people I've been friends with for years. I told Ana things that even my own teammates don't know about me. I told her about my parents, my childhood, asked her about her relationship . . .

That was stupid on my part. There was no point bonding with her over some stupid game of twenty questions. She isn't going to be here long. Most likely, she'll eventually go back to Kress. And even then, I couldn't bring myself to regret the conversation. Yeah, I revealed more than I wanted to, but just the chance to keep her big brown eyes directed at me had felt pretty damn good.

If that makes me a pussy, so be it. I haven't enjoyed the conversation of a woman in a long time. And even back then, none of them could hold a candle to Ana. Sweet. Generous. Kind. Beautiful, though she doesn't know it, which is really the best kind of beauty.

I enjoyed a handful of years in my youth where I sampled what was offered. Puck bunnies, or whatever you want to call them—the women eager to share the bed of a professional hockey player just to say they've done it. But after a while, it started to get stale, because it wasn't really *me* they were interested in. It was fleeting, carnal pleasure they were after, the chance to say they'd fucked a hockey player. They didn't ask about my childhood or my goals, or what I want out of life after hockey. But Ana did.

And, *God*, that lasagna . . .

After pouring myself a large mug of coffee, I carry it into the living room, grabbing my phone on the way, and then settle onto the couch. Just as I'm following up on an appointment I made yesterday, the front door opens to reveal Ana—dressed in a bright pink fleece sweater and black yoga pants. Hobbes barrels in between her legs and runs straight for me.

"Hi." She smiles when she sees me.

"Morning. There's coffee." I nod toward the kitchen.

"Perfect. It's chilly outside."

Rising briefly, I turn on the gas fireplace, which flickers to life with a soft whoosh. I rarely use the thing, but figure if she's cold, why not?

Ana's smile grows as she carries in her coffee to join me on the couch. "Oh, this is so cozy."

Hobbes flops to the floor with a huff in front of the fireplace.

"So I leave later today for a game on the East Coast," I say, swallowing a sip of coffee and looking at her over the top of my mug.

She nods. "The team flies out to New York. I know. I'll go stay with Georgia."

Jason's suspension means he isn't allowed on team premises, which includes the jet and games. But then he'll probably be here in Seattle, which also means there's no way in fuck Ana is going to stay at Georgia's. Kress went there once already looking for her. And if he did it again, this time I wouldn't be around to help her if things went south. I'd be three time zones away.

I shake my head. "You'll stay here."

Her eyes widen, appraising me. "Are you asking me or telling me?"

I clear my throat, shifting in my seat. "Right. Sorry. I just mean . . . it's no trouble having you here, and it's really the smart move. You, staying here for the time being."

If she leaves because I'm a surly asshole who doesn't know how to communicate, I'll feel even worse. It's not her fault I'm out of practice at this kind of thing.

She weighs my words, trying to determine if they're sincere. Then her gaze lifts to mine. "Are you sure you don't mind me being here when you're away?"

"It's really no problem. Plus, I like the idea of the place being used while I'm gone."

"Are you absolutely sure?"

"Positive."

Ana nods. "Then I guess I'll stay."

"Glad that's settled."

A knock at the front door grabs our attention.

"There's just one other thing," I say, rising to my feet.

Ana shoots me a curious glance. "Are you expecting someone?"

Nodding, I head toward the door. "I'm having a security alarm installed today before I go."

"Wait, what?" She jumps to her feet and follows me to the foyer with Hobbes in tow.

I open the front door to a trim man with a beard and blue tennis shoes. "Hi. Mr. Henry?"

"Yeah," I say. "But Grant's fine."

"Great. Well, I'm here to install your new security system, which should take about an hour."

"Come on in." I open the door wider and usher him in.

Ana's right on my heels as I follow the guy deeper inside my condo, where he begins unloading a small set of tools.

"I don't understand," she says, turning to face me. "Isn't Jason traveling with the team?"

I clear my throat and lead her into the hall where we'll have a little more privacy. "He's not. With the suspension, he's not even allowed on team property."

"Oh." Her face falls. "And you think he would . . ."

My throat tightens at the expression on her face. "No." Most likely he wouldn't try anything. Not now. At least, I hope not, but I clearly don't know the guy as well as I thought I did.

I still can't believe Ana spent two years with that fuck. I hate to think about what she went through. I may not know what love is, but I sure as hell know what love isn't.

"Is it not safe here? Is that what this is about?"

I reach out and place one hand on her shoulder. It's a touch meant to calm her, but instead, I can feel how tense she is. *Shit*. This is my fault. I never meant to make her feel on edge.

I drop my hand from her slender shoulder and shove it in my pocket. "No, it's nothing like that. I've just been meaning to do this for a while."

Her disbelieving gaze says she isn't so sure I'm telling her the truth.

"I just figured this might make you feel safer while I'm gone."

"It's only one night," she says, frowning.

"Yeah . . ."

"And I'm tougher than I look."

"I know," I say quickly.

She inhales, her nostrils flaring. Apparently, I answered too quickly. Now she doesn't believe I meant what I said.

"Let me do this one thing, Ana."

"It's your condo, Grant. I'm not going to stop you. But you've done a lot of things already."

"It hasn't been any hardship." That's the complete truth.

Looking uncomfortable, she shifts her weight. "Well, I promise to be out of your hair soon."

"I never asked you to leave." I meet her eyes, holding her gaze.

"No, you're too much of a gentleman to do

that."

I rub one hand over the stubble on my jaw. "Never been called that before."

Smiling, she softens. "Well, you are. I don't know what I would have done without you," she says quietly, her brown gaze holding steady to mine.

A moment of silence passes between us.

"You'd have figured it out."

She nods in agreement. "I suppose so."

And she would have. I'm sure of it, even if she's not.

"I have to leave in an hour, but I got you something." I grab a shopping bag from the top of the closet and hand it to her. As she starts to open the bag, I blurt, "It's bath salt. For when you use the bath in there."

She smiles up at me. "Thank you."

The guy from the security company calls out from the other room with a question, and I nod once to Ana and then head off.

An hour later, the security system is all set and the technician is gone. I grab my rolling suitcase from my room and stop in the living room where Ana is sitting on the floor with Hobbes.

"Hey. I'm going to head out. Otherwise, I'll be late and catch shit from the coach."

She looks up, her hand still lazily rubbing Hobbes's exposed belly. "Okay. Well, have a safe flight, and I hope you score a lot of goals."

I smile at her cuteness. "Thanks, I'll try my best. You remember the security code?"

She nods. "Yep, I've got it."

I grab the handle to my rolling bag, then pause when Ana rises to her feet and wraps her arms around me in an unexpected hug. Momentarily stunned—and totally unused to warm female affection—I stand there like a statue until she steps back, releasing me.

"Sorry," she says with a grin.

"Stay safe, okay?"

She nods, and with a slow exhale, I head to the door.

I make it down the elevator and into the parking garage when it hits me. I forgot my toiletry kit. I have no other choice but to go right back to my condo. Sighing, I place my bag in the car and make the trek back upstairs.

Unlocking the front door, I don't spot Ana on the floor with Hobbes anymore. He lifts his head and blinks at me.

As I head down the hall, I don't see any sign of her, so I call out, "Hey, I'm back. I just need to grab something."

No response.

That's weird. But, whatever, I really do need to get on the road.

I step into my bedroom and open the door to the adjoining master bath. And then my heart fucking stops.

Because standing in the center of my bathroom, completely naked and bent over to adjust the faucet, is Ana.

Creamy pale skin.

Full breasts.

The graceful curve of her lower back leading to a nicely rounded ass.

Oh my fuck.

As soon as she spins to face me, I slam my eyes shut, and Ana lets out a scream.

"I'm sorry." I hold up both hands, my eyes still firmly closed. "So fucking sorry."

I hear a whoosh of fabric as I assume Ana grabs a towel from the towel bar and secures it around herself.

"I'm good now," she says, her voice slightly panicked.

Opening my eyes, I notice the tub is filled with bubbles and steamy water, and I lower my hands to my sides. "I forgot my toiletry bag. I didn't know you were in here."

Her gaze darts from mine to the counter. She grabs the gray felt bag I left behind and shoves it at me.

"I'm sorry, Ana," I say firmly, hoping she knows I mean those words.

She nods and releases a shaky exhale. "It's okay."

And then I do what any man would do.

I turn and flee like a fucking coward.

CHAPTER SEVEN

A Sliver of Hope

Ana

My heart is still hammering away long after Grant closes the bathroom door.

I can't help but replay the mortifying moment over and over again in my head. Me, unsuspecting, leaning over the tub to test the water. Grant, distracted, beelining from the front door to *his* bathroom, only to find a butt-naked lady screaming bloody murder at him like he's some perverted intruder.

Did he know I was getting in the tub? Of course not. I'm just the house guest who's been inconveniencing him for a couple of days now. Well, now he's definitely thinking about that house guest, considering he just clearly saw her tits and ass ten minutes ago. *Dear Lord.*

I sit in the tub, stewing over it for so long that the water grows cold and my fingers get pruney.

It was an accident, Ana. You have to shake this off, or you can't expect him to do the same. Besides, it's only fair, after I saw him in his underwear that first night.

I perk up my ears, listening once more for any unfamiliar sounds, making sure that I really am the *only* one in this condo. Then, when I'm convinced the only sounds are those of an anxious Hobbes, his tiny feet pitter-pattering from the front door to the bathroom door and back again, I emerge from the water.

The air is cool, and my skin is covered with a fine layer of goose bumps, my nipples at attention. I'm cold, but my core is warm. There's a pulsing deep in my center, a little voice I haven't heard in a long time asking, *Hey, what's going on here?* I ignore the voice, reaching for a towel to pat myself dry. If I listen to that little voice, I'll end up getting back in the water to do something to myself that's entirely indecent.

After I get dressed, I do a load of laundry and then make myself an early dinner. While I wait for my grilled cheese sandwich to cook, I have to admit it does give me a nice sense of satisfaction knowing the alarm system is set. Even if I do feel a little guilty that Grant installed it just for me—despite what he said.

I try to watch a movie, but I'm so distracted, I hardly absorb a word of it. Abandoning the movie halfway through, I head to the guest room. After folding my laundry, I slip into my pajamas and snuggle up in bed with Hobbes. I'm not sure how Grant feels about dogs on the furniture . . . that strikes me as something we should have talked about. But Hobbes is so at peace, curled up against my side, I don't have the heart to push him off.

I pull out my phone, ignoring all the missed calls and texts from Jason, and pull up Grant's contact. With deft fingers, I type out my message.

```
I'm safe. All locked in.
```

In less than a minute, my phone buzzes. Almost like he was about to text me himself.

```
I'm so sorry I just barged in
            like that earlier.
```

I chuckle, appreciating how sensitive he can be.

```
It's your bathroom! Plus, I saw
you in your underwear the night
```

before, remember? Now we're
even.

My heart nearly jumps out of my throat when the message screen suddenly lights up with a call from Grant, and my phone vibrates aggressively in my hand. I pick up immediately, clearing my throat.

"Hello?"

"Hey, I'm not much of a texter. Is this okay?" His voice is somehow even lower and more gravelly over the phone.

"This is fine. What are you up to?" I ask, suddenly conscious of how my own voice sounds. *A little too . . . excited?*

"We just got done with team dinner. Some guys are heading to the bar, some to bed."

"That's good . . . and Jason isn't there?"

"Right."

Wow. They really did it. They really suspended him.

"Did anyone say anything about it?" I ask, twirling a lock of hair around my finger.

"No, no one that I could tell. I only really talked to Jordie at dinner, to be honest. But there's no way anyone knows you're staying at my place. I mean, I haven't told anyone."

"Thank you for that." A warm smile spreads across my lips. It's funny, but I don't think I ever specifically asked Grant to keep it a secret. He just knew. Knew that I needed to be guarded, kept safe from the world. "I appreciate everything you've done for me. I won't be in your hair for much longer, I promise."

He's quiet for a moment. "I never asked you to leave."

My breath hitches, and I pray he doesn't hear it. *At least he can't know how hot my cheeks are.*

"Yeah," I murmur, uncertain of what else to say. Something deep in my heart grows warmer by the second, to the point where I'm afraid I'll boil over and say something dumb. *Something emotional.* Instead, I only say, "But I'm sure I'm cramping your style."

"Not at all." Grant's voice is softer now, gentler. He's aware of how much I hate to inconvenience him, but he's determined not to make it a big deal. He would never kick me out, even though I'm sure he'd prefer the privacy. *Exhibit A, the bathroom incident.*

I scoff. "Grant, come on. I'm not an idiot. A single guy like you? Captain of the team? I'm sure you've got puck bunnies lined up around the block, vying for your attention."

"Not really." He chuckles, seemingly surprised by my use of hockey lingo.

I have ears, and Lord knows Jason used to love to tell me about all the puck bunnies he used to spend his nights with.

"I'm not much for the bar scene, or wherever that stuff happens."

I laugh. *Who is this man?* I can't remember if I've ever seen Grant with a significant other at an event . . . not that I was really looking before.

"Even so, I'm going to figure something else out. You'll have your bachelor pad back in no time, I promise. It'll be easier on both of us."

I can hear a muffled sigh on the other end. "Ana, I'm not who you think I am. I'm not interested in . . ."

When the line grows quiet, my brow furrows and my lips turn down into a frown. *Interested in what? Puck bunnies?*

"Never mind," he says. "What I meant to say is that it's been really nice having you around these past few days."

My eyebrows shoot up, and I croak, "Really?"

"You cook. You make good coffee. And you give really good massages," he says, and I can hear his grin through the receiver. "Your dog is kind of a pain in the ass, but—"

"How dare you!" I gasp, involuntary laughter bubbling up from deep in my belly. "Hobbes loves you!" I turn to pet Hobbes, who sniffles next to me in his sleep. Undoubtedly dreaming about those horrible squirrels again, I'm sure.

"Does he?" Grant asks, making a low sound that vibrates through me. "Well, I guess he's not *that* bad."

"Gee, thanks. I'll have to tell him how highly you think of him." I snicker, running my fingers absentmindedly through the pup's wheat-colored curls. "I guess I'm relieved that you don't absolutely *hate* having us around . . . but I don't buy it. You can clearly cook for yourself. And you have that team masseur for regular massages."

"Thor?" Grant scoffs. "Thor is the fucking worst. I haven't let him touch me for at least two seasons now."

"That explains why you're so tense all the time," I say with a laugh. My cheeks are starting to get sore from smiling so much. I don't remember the last time I laughed so freely.

Somehow, talking on the phone is so easy with Grant. He seems more comfortable, probably relieved that I can't scrutinize every flicker of emotion he tries so hard to conceal behind that stoic exterior. I can't say that I'm not also enjoying the strange anonymity of it all . . . lying here in bed, so cozy and warm. The low throbbing in my center hasn't disappeared at all. Rather, it's grown since I picked up the phone to hear that husky voice on the other end. I don't know what in the world is happening to me, but I shut it down quickly.

"You're much better than he is. Some people don't have the magic touch," Grant says, interrupting my thoughts. "Now you know why I want to keep you around."

I lick my lips. "So, are you saying that I have that magic touch?"

My voice is lower now, a little sultrier. This isn't my massage voice. No, this is my *flirting* voice—something a little darker and sweeter, dipped in bourbon and honey. And I'd be appalled at myself for using my flirty voice if I weren't having so much fun. Grant's chuckle on the other end of the line soaks my heart in buttery warmth, and I sink into the duvet with a happy sigh.

"You do. If you were a superhero, your power would be just that. One touch, and even your worst enemy would melt into a happy puddle."

"Well, I only give massages to people I like," I say, realizing a moment too late that I've said too much.

"Then I'm honored." Grant's tone is careful, as if he's only saying half of what he's thinking.

Part of me wants to push him to spill the beans, and the other half is perfectly okay with unspilled beans at this point in our friendship.

Friendship. I guess it is. Before, we were acquaintances at best, but I realize that's changed these past couple of days.

"You've been a really, really good friend, Grant," I say, suddenly overwhelmed with the desire to tell him how kind he's been to me. "Thank you for caring."

"You make it easy," he says softly, and my eyes

immediately prick with hot tears.

I didn't realize how badly I needed to hear that. After years of the kind of love that made me tired from the deepest parts of my soul, I always assumed there was something about me that made it difficult to be with me. *Difficult to care about me.*

"You should tell that to Jason," I say with a sigh. A joke in poor taste, maybe, but I can't help it. I'm so comfortable talking to Grant. The words come easily. Even those about my dick ex-boyfriend.

"If I ever see Jason again, I don't think we'll do much talking," Grant grumbles, and I giggle, smiling like an idiot again. It's nice to have a protector for a change.

"I appreciate that, but please don't do anything—"

"I wouldn't."

"I know."

The line is quiet for a few moments, and I can feel my heart pounding again. I have this urge to tell him something about myself that no one knows, something personal. *Something that matters.* But what would I tell him that I haven't already? I've already told him about my mom . . . about losing her. I haven't told many people about that part of me.

As if he reads my mind, Grant's voice fills my ear once again. "It's raining here. How's the weather over there?"

My heart swells. I know he's asking because he's thinking about how I can't sleep when it's storming at night. *Because of what happened to my mom.*

I take a moment to listen for rain on the windows, covered now by heavy, dark blue curtains, before responding in a quiet whisper.

"No rain here. I wouldn't be able to hear it anyway, over the dog's snoring." I wince, scrunching my eyes closed. *Dang.* "He's in bed with me . . . is that okay?"

"Yeah, why?" Grant's answer is immediate and laced with confusion.

"Some people don't like the smell of dog on the furniture. Dirt, and whatever," I say, which is odd enough in itself. *Did he really not think about this when he allowed a rambunctious little furball into his home?*

"Oh, I don't care at all. We had a dog when I

was growing up. Ruby slept on the couch."

"Ruby?"

"She was a yellow Lab. My mom and dad adopted her shortly after they adopted me. I wasn't that social as a kid."

"Oh, really? You weren't?" I tease, curling my toes into the sheets.

"I know. I did a real one-eighty as an adult, didn't I?" Grant chuckles.

We're both dissolving into laughter when I hear an unfamiliar voice on the other end, calling for Grant.

"I'm on the phone. Hold on." His voice is distant for a moment, like he's holding the phone away from his mouth to respond to this mystery person.

I bite my lip. I don't want this phone call to end.

"Sorry," Grant says. "That was Jordie. I guess he found me."

"Were you hiding?"

"Something like that." Grant chuckles again.

I really love that sound. It's deep and rumbly, and slices right through me.

"Well, I'll let you go, then," I say, ignoring the subtle ache in my chest. *Time to be a grown-up.* I can't spend all night giggling on the phone with a boy, like we're hormonal teenagers.

Grant sighs, and I can imagine him scrubbing his face with one hand like he does. "Yeah, you're probably right. Big game tomorrow. Probably should attempt to get some sleep."

"Good luck," I say, meaning it with my whole heart. *He deserves to win.*

"Thank you, Ana," he says, and I commit to memory the sound of my name on his lips. "Sleep well, okay? And call me if you need anything."

"I will. Good night, Grant."

"Good night."

We hang up, and I let my phone drop onto the bed.

Hobbes snaps awake with a jolt, surprised by the movement. I apologize to him with a soft kiss on his wet little nose, and he soon curls back into a fluffy mound against my side.

The bed is warm, embracing me in a cocoon of cotton and silk. I'm thankful to have this little companion in my bed, even if he does have paws.

And the assurance that Grant is only a phone call away gives me comfort too. He's an interesting man, and the more I learn about him, the more I want to know.

I've always assumed strength is loud. That the loudest voice in the room belongs to the strongest person. But with Grant, I'm learning strength can be silent too. Because his quiet and thoughtful approach is the most dignified thing I've ever seen.

That quiet strength communicates so much more than words ever could. His expressive gray eyes say that he'll catch me when I fall, that I'm really welcome here, despite my anxiety that tells me otherwise. That he doesn't blame me for finding myself in such a disastrous relationship. With everything I've been through lately, it means a lot to know that someone believes in me.

It's with those comforting thoughts that I slip into a peaceful slumber.

CHAPTER EIGHT

Coupling Up

Grant

"And then she made me promise I wouldn't tell anyone," Asher says with a chuckle.

Well, it's safe to say the cat's out of the bag on that one. The topic of tonight's conversation? The time one of the rookies, Landon, witnessed Asher's fiancée giving him a blow job.

God, I swear my teammates are idiots.

We're at the bar now, and even though we can't partake in anything stronger than soda and lemonade the night before a game, we'll be damned if we go to bed before curfew.

But their weird sex stories are actually an improvement over the dinner conversations I was forced to endure. At the team dinner tonight, there was a whole lot of wedding talk. My teammate Teddy and his former fiancée and now brand-new wife, Sara, just eloped. And another teammate of mine, Justin, is planning a wedding to his long-time girlfriend, Elise. Owen's married now, and Asher is engaged. Only the couple of rookies are still single—well, and me, of course.

I always feel so alone during these discussions with nothing to contribute to the conversation besides some well-timed nodding.

But tonight something feels different, because all I can think about is the fact that I do have a woman living in my apartment right now, however temporary that might be. Still, I like the thought that I have someone to come home to after this trip. I wonder if my place will smell like her, or maybe like buttery French toast again. I find myself smiling at the idea of that.

I always figured I'd be married by now, maybe even have a couple of kids filling the bedrooms of a big house in the suburbs. A big backyard with touch football games, and barbecues, and lemonade. It's what I pictured when I was younger, what I hoped for. But at thirty-two, I'm still single and living alone in a condo. My teammates are my family, and while most of them are years younger than me, they're all starting to find someone special and get married. It's something I try not to dwell on often.

My phone conversation with Ana earlier still swirls in my head, making it difficult to focus on the conversation around me.

I know she thinks she's in the way, but the truth is, I like knowing she's there. Like just having another human in my place. I love how she's made herself at home in my kitchen, love the way her nose scrunches up when her dog does something naughty. I like the sound of her laugh, and the way she hums to herself when she cooks. She's so domestic and nurturing, even with that damn dog. I know she'll make a great wife someday to a lucky man. It's a hard idea to swallow, because I also know that man won't be me.

God, the image of her standing naked at the bathtub is one I won't soon forget. Pale curves and full breasts . . . my hands itched to touch her. I wouldn't, of course. Couldn't.

"What do you think, Grant?" Jordie asks, pulling my attention back to the conversation.

"About what?"

He sighs, shaking his head. "About what will

happen to Kress once his suspension is up?"

That's a great question, and one I have no answer to. In the meantime, there's one thing I know for sure.

I'll do my damnedest to keep Ana safe.

CHAPTER NINE

Giving In

Ana

The following night, I find myself in Grant's bed. His sheets smell just like him—clean and earthy, reminding me of the night air right after a brutal storm. Unfortunately, the storm outside still rages, with no promise of letting up anytime soon.

Memories of that fateful night flash with every bolt of lightning, totally wreaking havoc on any sense of calm I've achieved. I'm too old to be afraid of the dark, but that doesn't change the fact that I am. I see death and destruction lurking in its shadows, and panicked feelings claw up my throat, tightening it like a noose. I should have outgrown this anxiety by now, and I'm ashamed that I haven't.

In the echo of each crack, I can still hear the phone ringing, the one next to the fridge in my family's kitchen. Then I hear the hurried shuffle of my dad's slippers from his post at the living room window to the phone. It was his crying that pulled me out of bed, and I tiptoed on cold toes to the kitchen.

I will never forget Dad's near-animalistic wailing, or the sight of him crumpled on the linoleum floor. I'd never heard him cry before that night. I would later learn that Mom's car was crushed by the impact of another vehicle, the roads slick with freezing rain. All I knew in that moment, though, was that something was terribly wrong.

When the storm began around nine o'clock this evening, I managed to stay bundled up with Hobbes in the guest room for the first hour of rainfall. But then lightning began painting the room white in violent strokes. So, with trembling hands, I carried Hobbes with me to Grant's bedroom, which is larger and somehow cozier with a big fluffy king-size bed and a soft wool rug on the floor. And since he isn't home, I didn't see the harm in camping out in here for a little while until the storm passes.

After setting Hobbes down on the dark blue duvet, I rushed to the sole window in his room to close the heavy curtain, muffling the roaring thunder behind a single pane of thin glass and, *thank God,* the thick drapes. Once I snuggled into bed, I caught Grant's scent on the pillow, masculine and with a hint of spice from whatever products he uses. Wrapped in his sheets, I suddenly felt protected. *Strange how comforting this smell is.*

Now, at least an hour has passed. I'm beginning to doze off, my nose tucked under the sinfully soft sheets. I find myself savoring every inhalation of Grant's comforting shampoo. *Or is it body wash?* There I go again, thinking about him in the shower . . .

Click.

My eyes flutter open, adjusting to the sudden light in the corner of the room. *What time is it?*

Grant is home, his broad shoulders silhouetted against the bright interior of the walk-in closet. After a few blinks, I can make out the full form of his body, removing the suit he's required to wear while flying with careful, quiet motions. He moves as silently as he can, trying not to wake me.

Oh no . . . how long have I been asleep? From the way his sheets are twisted around my legs and my dog is nowhere to be seen, it's been hours.

I would be embarrassed, but I'm too awestruck to care. I haven't slept through a storm in . . . at least a decade. Usually, the best I can do is pop a sleeping pill and hope the nightmares don't leave me with muscle tension in the morning.

Amazingly, the rain still pours outside, but the thunder is only a low rumble. The little girl in me wants to dive back under the duvet and snatch a few more hours of peaceful sleep, but the adult knows I need to give Grant his bed back. *And apologize.*

I sit up, and Grant must hear me rustling in his bed because he turns around.

"I'm sorry," he murmurs softly, his eyes wide and his hands hovering over the buttons of his dress shirt.

Through the opening of the shirt and the way the rain-drenched fabric clings to his chest, I can make out every delicious muscle. Even in the dim light of the room, I'm taken with how strikingly handsome this man is. *Beautiful, even.*

"No, I'm sorry," I say, clearing my throat. "I wasn't sleeping well in the guest room because of the storm." I swing my bare legs over the side of the bed, rubbing the sleep out of my eyes.

Grant glances at the drape-covered window,

then takes a step toward me. "I figured." He nods, gesturing to the door. "I was going to crash on the couch. Just need to change. You can stay right there."

My lips part. I close my eyes with a resigned sigh, my gaze downcast.

I can't shake the feeling that I'm taking advantage of him. I've disrupted his world with my personal problems, and now I have the audacity to sneak into his bed?

When I open my eyes, I see Grant's sock-covered feet cross the wooden floor to the side of the bed, where he stands over me. I can't bear to meet his eyes. *I don't know what will come out of my mouth if I do.*

"Are you all right?" he asks, his hands at his sides.

Thunder cracks outside, and I jolt involuntarily. I don't have time to kick myself for my skittishness because I'm suddenly staring into two warm eyes, my shoulders held tightly in his hands as Grant kneels down before me. I feel so incredibly naked right now . . . even more so than when he actually saw my naked body.

"Hey, what can I do?" he asks, his eyes searching my face with a concern I never expected.

I have no idea what's come over me, but in this moment, I ache for his attention and care, after years of having neither. It's hard not to when he gives it so freely.

"Can you . . ." I hesitate, uncertain of what I'm about to suggest. "Can you stay in here?"

It's a bold question, but his eyes don't leave mine.

"I can't sleep after a game. I don't want to keep you up." His voice is soft, but deep.

"You won't," I say, scooting across the mattress. I pat the warm space on the bed next to me. "Would you just lay here for a while? Next to me?"

He seems to consider this for a moment. I'm certain he's going to come up with some excuse about respecting my space, or something equally as dumb and gentlemanly.

Instead, I feel the mattress give as he leans over the bed, carefully lying on his back so his body is across from mine, one hand sandwiched between his head and the pillow. He keeps a safe distance between us, his gaze glued to the ceiling, his expression unreadable.

"Thank you," I whisper, and I lie down on my side, the pillow cool against my cheek. I take a moment to stare at his profile now, memorizing the faint lines around his eyes, the sharp angle of his nose, the plump outline of his lips.

After a prolonged moment of silence, Grant's lips part. "Are you sure you're okay?" His voice is strained, like he's on edge about something.

I hope it's not me.

"I don't know," I say, my emotions floundering somewhere between fear and fascination. For as loudly as the rain beats against the window, the beating of my heart thrums even louder in my ears. "My mom died the night of a storm. They've bothered me ever since."

Bothered me are the words I use, but according to the therapist I saw for years afterward, it's actually anxiety. There are pills that could help me, but I never bothered taking them. They made me feel fidgety and weird.

"How can I help?"

Grant turns his face just enough so that his eyes can meet mine. I'm a buttery puddle in the warmth of his gaze.

"Hold me?" I rasp out the words without thinking.

The storm outside is like a faint memory. Now, the only sound I can hear is my blood pumping through my veins. *What am I doing?* Yes, having his arms around me will help, but I have no right to ask that of him.

"How?" he asks, unsure of what I want.

"Like this," I murmur, my hair dragging over the pillow as I lean into him, nestling my cheek against his broad chest.

The relief that sweeps over me is instantaneous, and I can't help but run my hand up his abdomen, resting it in the crevice between his firm pectoral muscles, my fingers playing with the buttons of his still-damp shirt. I sigh. He just feels so good.

For all of my nuzzling, Grant is incredibly still. I can't tell if he's even breathing. Maybe he's waiting for instructions? Permission?

"Put your arm around me," I whisper, my eyelids drooping.

He does, slowly, and before long, I'm locked in his firm but gentle embrace.

Oh my God. I don't realize I'm crying until a

tear drips down my nose and onto the collar of his shirt.

"It's okay to be scared," he murmurs, pressing his lips against my hair.

Grant's voice rasps pleasantly in my ear, and I nestle myself deeper into his arms with another shaky sigh. The simple, heartfelt act and his kind words comfort me more than I thought they would.

"You're safe. Breathe, sweetheart. You're safe with me. I'm not going to let anything happen to you."

I do, drawing in a long breath and releasing it just as slowly.

"That's it. Do it again for me."

I inhale again, breathing deeply so I can feel my rib cage expand, the fullness of my breasts brushing against his firm chest.

"If you need to talk," he says, his voice deep, "I'm here. I'm not good at that kind of thing, but I can listen."

"It's okay." I breathe out slowly. "I'm okay. Just hold me a minute longer?"

"Anything."

We stay like that for several minutes. The temperature in the room seems to rise until it's humid between us, the air thick with tension. And temptation. And something else I can't quite put my finger on.

My next words pour out of me like rain from a gutter. "Thank you. I don't know what I'd do without you."

When Grant doesn't respond, my fingers slide up his chest to his throat, and along the defined line of his stubbled jaw. With a shaking hand, I draw his face toward mine, our eyes meeting in the darkness of the room.

"Did you hear me?" I ask, my gaze flicking between his eyes and lips.

His tongue darts out to lick his lips, leaving a hypnotizing gleam. "Yeah." He breathes out, saying softly, "It's no pr—"

I bring my mouth to his in a breathless kiss, humility be damned.

Grant grunts low, his hand shooting up to catch my jaw with calloused fingers. His lips are sinfully soft against mine, and they move slowly, not asking for too much too soon. I press into him, my fingers curling into the hair at the nape of his neck with a desperation brewing in my belly that I haven't felt since . . . *maybe ever.*

I pull back, pressing my thumb to his lower lip. "Is this okay?" I whisper, praying that he says, *Yes, this is more than okay.*

Grant doesn't speak, his breathing ragged and slow. I rub my thumb across his full lower lip. He draws my thumb into his mouth, catching my fingertip on his teeth. I hold my breath as Grant slides his fingers into the curtain of hair draped over my collarbone, pulling it over my shoulder to reveal the length of my neck.

He moves deliberately and leans down to press his lips to mine in a slow kiss, his palm resting firmly on the junction of my neck and shoulder.

I sigh into his kiss, opening my lips to his seeking tongue. A whimper escapes my throat when he brushes the outline of my ear with his fingers, and a current of electricity runs from the top of my head down to my toes.

Acting on instinct, I pull him on top of me, relishing the way his broad body covers mine. He's careful not to crush me, but I don't want careful. I lift my hips off the mattress to grind into his, his belt buckle brushing deliciously against my most tender spot. Grant releases a groan, dropping his lips to my neck. I allow my eyes to flutter closed, drunk on his hot breath against my sensitive skin.

"Please," I whisper, when Grant's lips pause against my skin in a moment's doubt.

Please don't stop now.

CHAPTER TEN

Hot and Heavy

Grant

This is *not* what I expected when I arrived home tonight.

First, finding Ana in my bed . . . then lying with her, holding her, comforting her. It should feel foreign, strange—wrong. But it doesn't. It feels amazing. She fits against me perfectly, molding her slender body to mine, nestling herself in against my chest, like I alone have the power to ease her discomfort.

My intentions were innocent—at first.

When I saw her reaction to the storm, I only wanted to provide comfort. Although it's out of the ordinary for me to play that role for someone, somehow it miraculously worked. Ana relaxed against me, her breathing evening out. But then she turned her face to mine and offered up those lips, and all my self-control unraveled.

Because kissing her . . .

God, it's the perfect kiss. Wet and hot and searing.

It's been so long since I've held a woman in my arms, had a woman in my bed . . . So, yeah, my body reacts, immediately hardening, even though I will it not to.

And then when Ana pulls me on top of her, all my reservations vanish like a bolt of lightning in the night sky.

I hover over her, my body caging hers beneath mine with my forearms balanced on the bed near her head. She's so small, so fragile, and it takes some effort to keep the bulk of my weight from crushing her.

She makes a low noise of contentment, and my heart shudders. Knowing that she trusts me to care for her, that it's my chest she's buried herself into, that it's me she wants comfort from? My chest gets so tight I can hardly breathe, and I press a soft kiss to her temple.

Settling myself over top of her, I tilt her chin to

mine and deepen our kiss. Ana's hips lift, seeking friction against mine. A gasp escapes her perfect mouth as my lips travel to her throat. She smells so good, and tastes even better.

Her hands ball into fists against my shirt, her pulse thrumming fast. She nuzzles right into the hollow of my throat, her smooth cheek brushing over my stubbled one.

She shifts, moving against me, and I swallow a groan when her fingers graze the growing bulge behind my zipper.

"Ana . . ." I rumble out the warning, barely breathing. She has to know she's turning me on. Has to know this is too far. I have a gorgeous woman in my bed—something that hasn't happened in a very long time. My self-control is far less reliable than I'd like right now.

I need to tell her to stop, need to put some distance between us. Of course, I do none of those things.

"Grant," she murmurs, her lips touching my skin.

Fractures of heat flash through me and my cock stands at full salute. I groan as her pelvis rubs enticingly against mine.

"Tell me," I say, leaning closer to brush my lips across her neck.

"I need you," she whispers, trembling in my arms, but for an entirely different reason than before. Delicate hands push against my clothes, trying to work them open.

Her eyelids flutter closed as my brain screams at me to end this. But I won't. I can't. I'm too far gone to care that this is wrong. I'm powered now on blinding need and the thrill of discovering every inch of this beautiful girl.

Our mouths meet in a kiss that's so hot and urgent, I groan out of relief. Ana's tongue seeks entrance, and I devour her mouth with deep, drugging kisses that make me feel drunk.

"Tell me if you want to stop. We don't have to do anything that . . ."

The words die in my throat and a deep rumble takes its place because Ana is undeterred, her hand pushing inside my dress pants. I forget how to breathe when it slips under the elastic of my boxer briefs. I'm hard as a fucking rock, and there's not a thing I can do about that.

"Wait, sweetheart, wait . . ." *Fuck.*

Her touch is electric, and I shiver at the contact. It's been a *really* long time since someone other than me has touched my dick.

"Do you not want to?" she asks on a strained exhale.

She's lovely. And beautiful. Of course I want to.

"Are you kidding? Do whatever you want to me."

"Oh God . . ." She moans as her fingers curl around my shaft.

My chest shudders at the contact of her delicate palm stroking me, and again at the sound of the whispered curse tumbling from her perfect mouth.

"Grant, you're so big," she murmurs, her breath coming out in quick puffs against my throat. "Please. I need this. I need you."

Throwing common sense out the fucking window, I move, changing our positions so I'm lying beside her. I need to see her eyes. Need to know what she's thinking. Need to be sure this is okay.

"You sure this is what you want?" My words are little more than a harsh pant.

Her mouth is nuzzling the stubble on my jaw in the most distracting way ever. "So much."

Jesus. How can I be expected to think with anything but the head below my belt?

I want her. From the first moment I laid eyes on Ana a year ago at a Hawks game, I've wanted her. As wrong as that was, especially because she was in the WAGs box at the time. She was taken. By one of my own damn teammates. And still, I wanted her.

Does that make me a douche? Maybe, but I never acted on it. Never showed even a flicker of interest toward her. Not when I first shook her hand, not when I made small talk with her at a charity event several months later, not when I drove her home for the first time after Jason had a meltdown at our friends' going-away party, and not even when I gave her a ride home from the start-of-the-season banquet. My one faux pas? Giving her my phone number. But even that was innocent. I had the strange suspicion that there might come a day when Ana needed a hand.

But now?

Now that she's pushing her lower body against mine in a slow grind—it's game over. I'm done.

I can't resist her any longer. Nothing and no one is standing in our way now. We're just two adults with a whole lot of chemistry and pent-up sexual desire.

I bring my mouth to hers again and capture her lips in a slow, sweet kiss. Ana's tongue reaches out to confidently stroke against mine. When I run one hand along the side of her rib cage and stop at her breast, she moans. I pinch her nipple between my thumb and forefinger, and she jolts, her pelvis bumping into mine urgently as we lie side by side.

"Please," she whispers against my lips.

Working my fingers into the side of her sleep shorts, I find her wet for me already. Although I only meant to tempt, to tease, when she lets out a long, breathy groan, I sink two fingers into her warm heat. Her voice goes molten, her moan melting like warm honey as her pliable body accommodates me.

"Yeah. There," she whispers, shuddering against me.

I can't get enough of touching her. The sounds she's making. The way she feels in my arms.

Lifting her off the bed for a second, I pull her shorts and panties down her hips until she can shimmy out of them. Ana unbuttons my pants and I begin working on my shirt. Soon we're both naked, and *fuck*, I'm going to embarrass myself. She's so sexy and gorgeous, and also so small. I'll need to be careful.

But Ana's not careful. Not with the way she pulls at my shoulders until I'm on top of her again, not with the way she kisses me or grinds herself against my hard cock. I can feel how wet she is, and my entire body shudders.

Eagerly, she grasps me in her right hand and guides me to her center. At my hesitation, she whimpers. "Please." And then she's gripping my ass muscles as I thrust forward.

Overcome by a kick of desire so fierce, I have no choice but to respond.

I may be the one on top, but Ana is the one calling the shots. With her murmured praise, she directs me. With her body's response to my hard, deep thrusts and her cries of pleasure, she lets me know when I find the right spot. The electrified gasp she makes when my fingers find her clit urges me on.

With each slow, even stroke, Ana loses her self-control. She moans and tilts her hips to erase any remaining distance between us, and I can't get enough. She feels so good. Wet and hot and wonderful.

Her breath comes faster against the hollow of my throat until she comes apart, quaking beneath me and clinging to my shoulders with a final soft cry of pleasure.

A couple more pumps and I follow her over the edge, emptying myself inside her.

Afterward, I hold her and wait for regret to come. But it doesn't. There's only a deep sense of satisfaction and an unfamiliar softness inside my chest.

That was fucking intense. And perfect. And so hot.

The feelings of regret come later. Or more specifically, in the morning when I wake and find the bed next to me empty.

CHAPTER ELEVEN

Time to Focus on Me

Ana

Standing in front of the guest bathroom mirror and wearing nothing but a towel, I take in my flushed cheeks and tangled hair.

Last night was unexpected, and yeah, a little crazy, I can see that now. It was hot and passion-filled, and at the same time, tender. More tender than I expected sex to be with such a huge, brooding man.

But Grant's body moved with the confidence of an experienced lover, wringing every last ounce of pleasure from me before finally letting himself go—with a delicious low-sounding grunt and a deep rumbling groan. The feel of his stubble against my skin, the way his teeth grazed my neck right before he climaxed . . . His big body positioned over mine, his impressive length stretching me with a welcome sting. The memory of it makes my inner muscles clench in tribute to how amazing the sex was.

All I wanted in that moment was for him to erase every ugly memory that had clouded my brain over the past week. And I was so greedy, taking first the comfort that he offered, and then pleasure. So much pleasure, it was blinding—all consuming. The best sex of my life, which I try not to focus on because I'm not sure it's ever going to happen again.

Sex with Jason was good. But there was nothing merely *good* with sleeping with Grant.

First, he's huge—everywhere. I shiver even now at the memory of reaching beneath the elastic of his boxers for the first time. And second, he was so confident, so sure. The way he moved. The way he kissed me. With complete control and laser focus.

Dear God. I suck in a huge breath, ignoring the way my lower half tingles without my permission.

Okay, stop it, Ana. Nothing good can come from this. It was a one-time thing.

Grant's been so kind to me, a good friend. I'm

not going to use him as some meaningless rebound fling. And heaven knows I'm certainly not ready for something more serious than that, anyway.

I need to take the next few months as *me* time, time to clear my head and focus on myself, and that doesn't include jumping into the bed of my ex's teammate—no matter how deliciously sexy he is. But being near Grant makes my stomach knot with something hot and urgent. I'm confused about a lot of things, but my attraction to him isn't one of them.

Which is why I'll need to be extra vigilant about making sure we stay in the friend zone from here on out.

With that decision made, I feel more at ease, more clearheaded than I have in days. I run my brush through my hair, the first step to trying to put myself back together.

It's easier said than done.

CHAPTER TWELVE

Out of Practice

Grant

After spending the night with Ana in my bed, I awake in the morning to rumpled sheets and her scent on the pillow. She's gone.

I keep myself busy most of the day, first with a team skate, and then by dropping off a couple of bags filled with groceries at the local homeless shelter like I do every week. I consider going back to the store for even more groceries, but I can't stay out of my apartment forever.

I might be avoiding going home. Okay, I am. But I shouldn't have slept with Ana last night, and that's become glaringly obvious in the light of day.

But when I saw her huddled in my bed last night, her face tense in sleep, it twisted something inside me. I've seen guys unconscious on the ice after a brutal hit, seen players with broken bones and concussions and all types of serious injuries. But I've never seen someone look so helpless and desperate in their sleep.

The urge to crawl into bed beside her and hold her, even before she invited me to, was a sharp pulse of need. It goes without saying that I have no idea what I'm doing, because I'm not the guy you go to for emotional support or cuddling comfort. But for Ana, all I want in the world is the chance to see her smile again.

Deciding I can't stay away any longer, I turn my car toward home and dial Coach on the drive there.

"Hey, Grant," he says, answering on the first ring. It's almost like he was expecting me to call. Then again, maybe he was. We said we'd touch base today.

"Hey, Coach." I clear my throat, deciding to cut right to the chase rather than waste time on pleasantries. "Any word on Kress?"

"Actually, yeah, there's been a change."

When he hesitates for a moment, I'm suddenly terrified that he's going to tell me they've lifted the suspension and reinstated the abusive prick. If that happens, my days of being captain of this team will come to a swift and unfortunate ending. Because I'll be the one getting suspended, since I'm pretty sure physical violence against a teammate is frowned upon. And I've just been waiting for an excuse to beat Kress's ass from here to next Sunday.

Finally, Coach continues, and the next words out of his mouth are the last ones I expect. "He's been sent down." Which means he's being moved to our affiliate team in Wisconsin, two thousand miles away. *Holy shit.*

The news hits me like a fist to the sternum. Elation and relief settle over me, along with a sense of calm I haven't felt since this entire mess started. Maybe this will all turn out okay. Maybe Ana will get the fresh start she deserves.

"Copy that. Thanks for the update."

"Sure thing. Anything else?"

"Do you think she should, ah, press charges?" I say after a pause.

Rather than telling me to mind my own business like I half expect him to, Coach launches into a lengthy explanation about a conversation he had with the team lawyer. Apparently, even if Ana were willing to press charges, cases like this rarely go anywhere. Which is, of course, utter bullshit.

"It's up to her, of course," he says. "Just giving you my two cents."

With a defeated sigh, I grunt my acknowledgment. "Thanks, Coach."

"Anytime. Talk to you soon, Grant."

We end the call just as I reach my building. After parking in the garage, I make my way upstairs.

"Hello?" I call out into the empty condo. Hobbes runs over to greet me, but Ana's nowhere to be found. She must still be at work.

I obsessed over seeing her today, purposely staying out of my own home all day, and she's not even here. *Figures.*

After taking Hobbes out, I check the time. It's almost six. I'm not sure what shift Ana might have been working today, or when to expect her, but decide to go ahead and order us dinner. She could have plans with her friend . . . hell, she could have gone back to her ex for all I know. It's a thought that stings more than I want it to.

After ordering a couple of pizzas and a spinach salad, I toss my phone on the couch and wait. It's not long before Ana arrives, placing her purse onto the counter as she enters.

"Hey," she says in a cheery voice, meeting my eyes.

"Hey," I say back, my voice a little hoarse.

She opens her mouth to say something more, but the sound of the intercom buzzing distracts her.

"I ordered pizza," I say, pressing the button to grant the delivery person access to the building.

"Oh, that's perfect," she says. "I'll just take Hobbes out, and then—"

I hold up one hand. "Already taken care of."

Ana's mouth twitches with a smile. "You're too nice to me. Have I told you that already?"

Shaking my head, I chuckle at her. What was I so worried about earlier? Things don't feel any different between us. Unless you count the buzzing attraction I'm trying hard to ignore.

"It was nothing."

"Then I guess I'll go change and wash up for dinner."

I nod. "Sounds like a plan."

Wearing her usual work outfit of yoga pants and a shirt with the spa's logo, she heads off to change.

I'm not sure if I should address the elephant in the room and apologize for last night, but so far, Ana doesn't seem upset or bothered by the thing we did last night, so I stay quiet.

By the time she returns dressed in a different pair of yoga pants and a baggy T-shirt, I've got the pizza boxes open and two plates on the counter. She puts out a bowl of dog food for Hobbes, which he attacks with gusto.

"Help yourself," I say, nodding toward the spread on the counter.

"Thanks." She grins before taking a slice of each kind of pizza and a large portion of the salad.

We settle in side by side on my couch and dig into our food.

I glance her way. "So, last night . . ."

She bites her plump lower lip and her gaze darts over to Hobbes. "We don't have to talk about it."

I'm not sure what to make of her comment. Does she not want to talk about it? Or does she not want me doing so out of obligation?

I clear my throat and start again. "All right. Uh, how was your day?"

She launches into a story about a client she had today, a woman who was nine months pregnant and suffering from lower back pain. She thought she needed a prenatal massage, but it turned out she was in the early stages of labor. Ana waited with the client while she called her doctor, and then her husband.

Ana looks up at me, a slice of pizza in one hand. "What about you? Keep yourself busy?"

I nod. "Yeah. I, um, actually have a little bit of an update for you. I talked to Coach today."

"Oh." Her face falls. She's bracing for bad news, just like I did.

Clearing my throat, I push my plate away. "The suspension is still in place for seven more games, but Kress is moving down. He's headed to Wisconsin."

"Wow." Ana's shoulders drop as the news sinks in. "That's . . . unexpected."

Nodding, I touch her shoulder. "I know. But it's good news, right?"

"It is," she says quickly, meeting my eyes.

A zing of electricity bolts through me at the memory of last night. *Fuck.*

The sex between us was off-the-charts incredible. But we can't do that again. It was all kinds of inappropriate of me to cross that line. Still, I can't bring myself to regret it. Even if it's never happening again.

She works her bottom lip between her teeth while she considers the news that Jason is leaving. There's a brightness to her eyes I can't look away from.

Drop it, dude, she's not yours. Never will be.

Rising to my feet, I carry my plate into the kitchen. "I'm tired. Think I'm going to turn in early tonight."

Ana watches me with a curious expression from her spot on the couch. "Okay," she murmurs while Hobbes settles in by her feet, begging for a scrap of food.

"Good night," I say as I head off.

The truth is, I'm not even a little bit tired. I just don't trust myself to be alone with her right now.

Ana isn't my toy to play with, and I need to remember that.

CHAPTER THIRTEEN

It's Time to Be a Grown-Up

Ana

The stunned silence that settles around me after Grant flees to his bedroom under the guise of being *tired* is deafening.

I lift Hobbes from his sleepy spot by my feet and cuddle him to me. "You'll keep me company, won't you?" I murmur, pressing my face into his fuzzy little chest.

He looks at me and yawns.

Releasing a sigh, I set Hobbes down again.

Grant played it off well, but I could sense something was off from the moment I came inside tonight. He was strained and uncomfortable, and trying to put distance between us, like increasing our physical proximity would somehow quash the growing attraction between us. It didn't. Not for me. But that doesn't mean I'm not good at compartmentalizing. I don't have much choice.

I can't hop from one relationship to the next—from one hockey player to the next. *God, what would people say?* I have more dignity than that. I can practically hear the rumors flying now about how I'm sleeping my way through the team roster. And I won't be *that* girl.

Instead, I'm going to be the girl who gets her shit together, the girl who gets her life back on track and won't allow one asshole ex-boyfriend to sabotage all her plans. And just because Grant is a gorgeous, thoughtful man doesn't mean he's the right man for me. He provided a level of comfort and care last night that I didn't expect to need—but I did need it. And he freely gave it, generously and without judgment.

But I need to focus on myself and rebuilding my life. Simple as that. I can't let a moody, decidedly sexy man deter me from that goal.

• • •

The reflection staring back at me in the mirror makes a sour face.

I've worn this pink sweater twice a week since I started staying with Grant, and I don't even *like* this sweater that much. It was just the first thing I grabbed out of my closet that night when Grant swept me away to his condo. That and an assortment of yoga pants and spa T-shirts for work, one ill-fitting pair of jeans, and underwear of the unsexy variety. *Not that there's any occasion for sexy underwear.*

Grant's out of town, at another away game, and I might be sulking.

He's been a complete ghost since we slept together. It's like we're back to square one. Not conversationally, though. He's not withholding or being short with me. It's more of a physical distance.

He touched my shoulder last night, and I felt that same lightning shudder through my whole body again. But before I could blink, he disappeared. All I want is to talk to him about what happened between us, but I can tell he isn't ready to. That's what I get for crossing a boundary, I guess.

I tug at the sweater, willing it to fit me differently. When my phone buzzes, I open my messages distractedly. The name on my screen is like a swift kick to the gut.

Jason.

My ex hasn't texted me in days, so I thought he was finally letting go. He's being forced to move to Wisconsin, thousands of miles away. A huge demotion, to be sure, but at least he's still playing hockey.

Memories of Jason—the good ones—live in a dusty, sealed box, tucked away deep in the recesses of my heart. I haven't dared open that box since the first time he shoved me against a wall. But now that I have the assurance of thousands of miles between us, it feels safer to revisit them.

With a deep, steadying breath, I open the message.

```
Hey. I packed your things in
boxes. Georgia is coming to get
them for you today. I'm moving
to Wisconsin, so I ended the
lease early. Let me know if the
landlord harasses you. Bye, Ana.
```

My heart seizes, and I steady myself against the dresser. With numb fingers, I call Georgia.

"Hello?"

"Hi, Georgie."

"Hey, babe, what's up?"

"You going to my old apartment today?"

There's only a hint of a pause before she speaks again, her voice clear and cheerful. "Yep! Want me to steal anything?"

I smile, relieved as feeling returns to my fingers and legs. I'm so lucky to have this beautiful, thoughtful person in my life. "Nothing specific. Should I come with you?"

"You don't have to do that. I've got it covered. Well, me and Bertha." Bertha is what she calls her trusty Jeep Wrangler.

"But like, *should* I come?" I chew on my thumbnail, not even sure what I want her answer to be.

"Do you want to?"

"I don't know." I hesitate, considering her question.

"It might give you some closure."

"That's what I was thinking."

"Well, if you want to come, I was going to head over in about, uh, forty-five minutes? I could swing by wherever you are right now."

"Could you pick me up on the corner of 32nd and Harrison?"

"Whoa, ritzy neighborhood. That's where you've been staying?"

All Georgia knows is that I'm staying with another friend, and she's been an angel for not asking for more details. We both know that Jason would corner her if he suspected she knew anything.

"Yeah. Nice, right?" I chuckle. "I'll be ready. Can't have you moving all my crap by yourself."

"Okay, I won't stand in the way of your journey of healing," Georgia says, only half ironically. "But if you want to back out, even at the last second, I've got you. You hear me?"

"I hear you," I murmur, relaxing with a warm sigh. "I owe you a killer massage."

"You really do!" Georgia laughs, and I join her. We both know we'll never go through with it. "I'll let you go. See you soon!"

"'Bye, Georgie."

"'Bye, babe."

About five minutes early, I'm standing on the corner. The wind cuts through me, even on this temperate day, and I rub my hands together for a little extra warmth.

It seems weird, going empty-handed into a trade-off like this. I didn't take anything of Jason's with me when I left the apartment, not even anything he gave me. The teddy bear he got for me on our first date has a special place on the media shelf, next to my collection of rom-coms and Jason's video games. The necklace he gave me for my birthday last year hangs from the jewelry stand in the bathroom, only worn on special occasions. I have no idea what I'll do with them. Part of me hopes he just threw them out.

Soon, a gray Jeep is pulling in front of me and Georgia is rolling down her window.

"Get in, loser! We're going soul-cleansing," Georgia calls from the driver's seat.

I can't help but snicker at the reference to one of our shared favorite movies. Leave it to Georgia to make me laugh on a day like this.

"Love the outfit," she says. "It's very 'look how well I'm doing without you.' I dig it."

"Really?" I scoff, pulling my seat belt over my coat and chunky sweater. "I'm just excited to get my wardrobe back."

"Yeah." Georgia sighs, putting the car in drive. "Do you want to say anything to him when you see him?"

I think about this for a moment. Is there anything I haven't already said to him?

"I don't know. I guess I'm just trying to anticipate what *he'll* say to *me*."

"Ugh, I don't want to even guess. Do you think he'll beg for you back?"

"No." I shake my head solemnly. "He's too proud."

"I think he only liked you because you took care of him. But that's just my take," Georgia says with a shrug.

"Well, your take would be correct." I sigh. "I just wish I'd gotten out before it got . . . the way it did."

"Violent? Honey, you can't blame yourself for not *anticipating* violence. That's crazy. That shit's not normal. At least, not in my experience."

We sit in silence for the rest of the car ride. Truthfully, I'm grateful she's giving me the space to think.

I know I need to brace myself for the worst possible scenario. Jason could get angry and throw something, or worse, hurt one of us. And even though I don't think that will happen, my stomach is still tied in knots.

Grant would freak out if he knew I was doing this.

I frown. *Enough of that.* I don't need Grant's permission, just like I never needed Jason's permission. This is my life, and I'll be damned if I don't call the police next time I feel like someone's threatening it.

Pulling up to our old brick building is surreal. It feels almost like an out-of-body experience as we trudge up the steps. I never had Georgia over in the past, so this will be her first and last time at my old place. *So weird.* Luckily, she doesn't seem fazed by any of this. Instead, she steps confidently up to the front door and hits the buzzer for number 201. Despite the elements, the tiny card with our last names is still legible: KRESS/WALSH.

The door buzzes and Georgia pushes through, leading me upstairs. Walking down the hall gives me tunnel vision as memories of shattered glass and hollow screams ring in my ears.

The door to the apartment is cracked open. Georgia stops, turning back to me. I give her a weak smile when she reaches out to squeeze my hand. With my fingertips, I push the door the rest of the way open.

I almost don't recognize Jason when I see him. He sits on the edge of the couch, looking skinnier than ever. His eyes have dark circles beneath them.

"I didn't know you were coming," he croaks, his gaze flicking to Georgia, who stands like a prison guard at the door.

That's kind of what this feels like . . . *visitation*.

"I didn't want Georgia coming here alone," I say, impressed with the strength of my voice. To be weak in front of this man again . . . well, let's just agree that I'd rather die.

"Right." He sighs before standing, and it takes everything in me not to flinch as he moves closer to me. "Let me help you with the boxes."

There's at least half a dozen, filled with clothes, books, pots and pans . . . all proof that I ever called this sad home my own. I want to object to his offer, but more hands means we can get through this quicker.

The three of us carry boxes down the stairs, carefully maneuvering around one another. Georgia only takes her eyes off of me to watch Jason when he gets too close.

But my instinct when I first opened the door is right. Jason is smaller now. Weaker. I wonder how much of that is the stress of his demotion, poor nutrition, regret . . . and how much of it is just my perception of him. He seemed so much bigger when he was throwing me against a wall.

I'm pulling the rear hatch of the Jeep down when I sense Jason nearing me. Georgia's in the front seat, her eyes boring into us through the rearview mirror. I spin around. Jason is a foot away, and that's too close. I take a step back.

"Can we talk for a sec?" he asks, but doesn't try to move any closer.

Good.

"Okay," I say with a nod.

There's a silence, but I wait it out. If he wants to talk, he'll have to do the talking.

Jason doesn't even meet my eyes. Instead, he stares at my shoes. "I know I ruined things between us."

"Yes."

"I know. But . . . I just can't go on living knowing that you hate me."

"I don't, Jason." I sigh. This feels almost juvenile. It makes my skin crawl.

"It seems like you hate me . . ." He runs a hand through his hair and finally meets my eyes, his colored with sadness.

Ah, there's the manipulator I knew and loved to a fault. *I was wondering where he went.*

"I don't hate you. But I do think you need professional help."

He scoffs. "Like therapy?"

"Yes."

When he sees how serious I am, his expression softens.

"Yeah, you're probably right. Anyway . . ." He clears his throat. "I'm really sorry for . . . everything. You didn't deserve to be treated like that."

"No, I didn't. Get some help, Jason. Take care."

And with that, I turn, walk around the Jeep, and let myself into the passenger side. In the side mirror, I watch Jason shuffle back into the building.

"Are you okay?"

The warmth of Georgia's voice melts my icy defenses into a pathetic puddle. I scrunch my eyes closed as unexpected tears begin sliding down my cheeks. Smothering a hiccup with my hand, I shake my head. I'm not okay.

"Oh, Ana, I'm sorry. So sorry." Georgia coos softly, wrapping an arm around my shoulder.

It's an awkward hug, a car hug, but it's perfect. I'm crying at this point, Georgia's comforting words soothing me with the promise of acceptance and safety.

"I'm so sorry this happened to you. You're so strong, the strongest person I know. I'm so proud of you."

"I think I really loved him." I sob, choking on the words. "How could I have loved him when he hurt me like that?"

"You've got a big heart, lady. A big, selfless heart." Georgia sighs, smoothing my hair back from my wet face. "You deserve the world, and you're gonna get it. You hear me?"

I nod, stifling another hiccup. "I hear you."

"How about we drown our tears in some margaritas?"

"It's not even one o'clock," I choke out, my shoulders shaking with laughter.

"Oh, good. Maybe we can catch a brunch special. Mimosas then. Buckle up!" Georgia hollers something like a battle cry as we peel out onto the street, leaving all of that mess and hurt in the dust.

I roll down the window, letting the brisk air dry my cheeks. With every turn, the boxes in the back of the car rattle and crash against each other, but I couldn't care less.

I'm free.

CHAPTER FOURTEEN

Oh, Baby

Grant

I shouldn't be here today. I should have just mailed in that little regrets card and sent along a gift.

What the hell was I thinking? A baby shower isn't my scene. If I didn't know it before, that's become abundantly clear in the last five minutes.

Exhibit A is my star goalie, who's currently blindfolded and trying to determine the dirty diapers from the clean ones using only his sense of smell. Apparently, a few select diapers have been sprayed with something called fart spray from the gag store.

So far, I haven't ventured into the living room where the games are being played, preferring to stick close to the kitchen where there's good, normal things, like beer. And no fart spray. I'm not normally a big drinker, but based on the fact that two of my players just chest-bumped over their victory of dressing a baby doll faster than their fiancées, I'm thankful for beer. Beer is good. Baby showers are bad.

Ana looks at me from across the room, meeting my gaze with an uncertain look.

At least she came with me today. Honestly, she's the reason I'm here.

Ana seemed thrilled with the idea of coming here today. She showered and then blow-dried her hair into loose waves, which is different from the simple ponytail she usually wears to work, and she smells fucking fantastic. Then she took her time elaborately wrapping a large gift in yellow and pale green paper. That was my first clue that Owen and Becca don't yet know the gender of their baby.

Maybe I should have known that already. But to be honest, while he's one of my best players and a huge asset to the team, Owen and I have always been just teammates. Great teammates, don't get me wrong, but in terms of friendship, we never really got there. He's a life-of-the-party kind of guy and has a big circle of friends, as evidenced by the huge group that showed up for him today.

Good for him. He deserves it. I'm more of the loner type.

The normally broody center, Justin Brady, is racing to beat the clock as he diapers a doll, and the fun-loving Teddy King is grinning like a loon while he races him. The twenty-five-year-old rookie, Jordie Prescott, is sitting alone at the dining table nursing a beer. He's always solo to team events like I usually am. The only difference is today I came with Ana, which is obviously a temporary thing.

"Dude, get your ass over here and play," the blond six-foot-four center, Asher, says with a cocky grin. "Owen is kicking all our asses."

"Come on, Cap!" Teddy says. "Show 'em how it's done."

I groan out a non-reply. I may be the oldest one here, but little do they know I have no clue about matters related to babies—or anything domestic, for that matter. Yes, I occasionally cook for myself, but that's about the extent of it. I don't even do my own laundry.

Ignoring their pleas, I watch as Ana makes small talk with the mom-to-be, Becca, touching the round swell of her belly with a gleeful expression.

Something inside me twists at Ana's tender

smile. God, maybe I was being a dick by not wanting to come. She clearly needed this today. Needed to be surrounded by friends and hockey players playing goofy games. I let out a sigh and rub one hand over the back of my neck just as Jordie approaches.

"Hey, man," he says, stopping beside me.

"Hey," I say, giving him a chin lift.

"Crazy news about Kress, huh?" His voice is low, his gaze drifting toward Ana. "Is she okay?"

He must have seen the footage on the news. Everyone did, I'm sure. Which is why it's even more important that everyone treat her as usual today. I wouldn't want anyone walking on eggshells or making her feel self-conscious. And so far, so good.

"Well . . ." I clear my throat, stalling. "First, it's her business. But she's a strong girl, and yeah, I think she's going to be just fine."

Jordie nods. "Understood."

After cupcakes have been eaten and gifts have been opened, I pause beside Ana, careful to keep some physical distance between us. There's no sense in getting my body confused, and we probably both prefer to keep our friends in the dark about what happened between us the other night.

As far as anyone knows, Ana and I only rode together today. They don't know we're living together, and I want to keep it that way.

"You about ready to get out of here?" I ask her after a few more people filter out and the party winds down.

She looks up at me with a softness in her eyes and nods. "Sure."

Becca hugs us both at the door and tries to get us to take some of the extra cupcakes. We both politely decline.

On the way home, Ana's quiet, calmly looking out the passenger window as I drive. I've got something I need to tell her, but decide to wait until we reach my place.

"Today was fun," she says, breaking the silence after a few minutes. "Owen is so extra." She grins, probably recalling the silly baby-shower games.

"Yeah," I murmur, chuckling.

"I'm so happy for Owen and Becca." She smiles. "They're going to make wonderful parents."

If only she could have seen Owen in his playboy heyday. He was quite the hedonist. But, yeah, married life has certainly been good for him.

A few minutes more and we reach my place. When I unlock the door, Hobbes comes running over.

"I'm gonna get someone to move these to the basement for you," I mutter as we step around the boxes stacked in the foyer.

Ana sighs and places one hand on her hip. "I know you're not happy I went over there when you were gone," she says, seeing right through my short tone. "It was my decision. And I wasn't alone."

I lick my lips and nod. "I'm sorry. You're right."

Ana has already lived with one controlling jerk, and I don't plan on being the second. It's *her life*, and these are *her* things. She had every right to go and get them.

Regardless, I wish I could have gone with her.

Now that I think about it, though, that would have been a terrible idea. I would have had no reason not to kick Kress's ass now that he's not a member of my team. Still, I could have at least sent a packing and moving company. Something.

Pausing in the kitchen, I run one hand over the back of my neck. "So, listen, can I talk to you about something?"

"Of course." She meets my eyes, waiting.

Her lips are perfect. I can't stop my brain from replaying our first kiss. It was hot and tender, and of course I want to kiss her again. *Not happening, dude.*

"Coach asked me to pick a cause for the team to support this season. Last year, it was breast cancer awareness, and all the guys changed the laces on their skates to pink ones. But for this year, I had another idea."

"Okay?"

"It's another women's cause, but I wanted to run it by you first."

"What is it?" she asks.

"Domestic violence."

I read a bunch of statistics online and was prepared to rattle these off to her—like that most violence against women is never reported to the police, or that one out of five murder victims is killed by an intimate partner. But it now seems really insensitive, so I keep my mouth shut.

"There's a women's shelter in Seattle that's vastly underfunded." I swallow the words as an unexpected wave of emotion sweeps through me. "We'd be donating a portion of ticket sales to help out."

Tears form in Ana's eyes, and she blinks them away. "I think that's amazing, Grant." Her voice is small and hushed.

I can't tell if she's touched by this or saddened by it. I'm still not good with crying, but I'd like to think I'm getting better.

Opening my arms, I beckon her closer. "You look like you could use a hug."

Softening, she smiles and steps into my embrace. "I didn't take you for the cuddly type. But look at you, exceeding all expectations."

"Trust me, I'm not."

"Could have fooled me," she murmurs, lingering in my arms. The top of her head doesn't even reach my chin, and her face is pressed into the front of my shirt.

It feels so good to hold Ana again. I haven't touched her since that night, not even an accidental bumping of elbows in the hallway. Nothing.

My heart rate picks up, and I take a step back at my body's response to hers being so close. "I'm sorry."

She blinks up at me. "For what?"

"I just . . ." I shove one hand in my pocket and force the words out of my mouth. "As perfect as the other night was, and believe me, I'm grateful you chose to share that with me . . . I don't think that can happen again."

She's quiet for a second, and then looks up to meet my eyes. "I'm not looking to jump into another relationship, Grant. You don't have to worry. It felt good. I think we both needed that. It doesn't have to mean anything."

I nod along to her little monologue, but she's wrong. It meant a lot more to me than it did to her, and that's why I won't let myself go there again. Because I can see how easy it would be to feel messy, inconvenient things for her, and how easily she could break my heart.

I'd like to smile and make a joke. I'd like to tell myself that sex between us could be casual and fun, and promise her that it wouldn't complicate things. But that would be a lie.

There's nothing simple about my feelings for

Ana. I don't normally do complicated, yet here I am, in way over my head with this girl.

• • •

When I walk into the dressing room the next morning, the sight before me shouldn't be a surprise. But it is. Because Jason shouldn't be here, yet here he is, standing there cleaning out his stall while the rest of the team gets changed for practice.

I guess I figured he'd sneak in at some off hour and do it without an audience. Or hell, even make one of the PAs clear it out for him and ship his shit to him. I haven't seen his face since the suspension started, and I'd started to convince myself that I never would.

"Hey, good luck in Wisconsin," one of the rookies says to him.

Jason nods. "It's all good."

"You're in a good mood," someone else says.

Jason chuckles and continues packing up his hockey bag, tossing in a pair of old socks. "I'm still going to be playing hockey, even if it is in the minors for a bit. Plus, I got laid this morning, and then had a long shower and a strong cup of coffee. Life is good, man."

My nostrils flare, and I tighten my hand around the roll of athletic tape I'm holding.

He's already fucking someone else?

What woman in her right mind would want anything to do with his sorry ass?

He could be bluffing—everything else in his life is falling apart at the moment. He lost his girlfriend, his spot on the pro roster, and has been disgraced by the media.

Even if he isn't bluffing, I really don't give a rat's ass. He's done hurting Ana as far as I'm concerned. And she won't hear about this from me. Somewhere along the way, protecting her has become something I do on instinct.

And I'll keep right on doing it, no matter the cost.

CHAPTER FIFTEEN

Deep Breaths

Ana

"**A**na?"

My eyes shoot open, the soft lighting of the massage parlor's ceiling slowly coming into focus. There's a carpet-like texture against my skin . . . wait, yep, I'm on the floor.

What the hell?

"Are you okay?" Almost in slow motion, Georgia slides into my vision. She's at my side, one hand on my shoulder and the other digging in her pocket.

"What happened?" I ask, my brow furrowed as I try to figure out what the hell happened. An older woman is half lying, half leaning over the massage table, staring at me with wide eyes, and my hands are slick with oil. *Oh shit.*

"You collapsed during a session," Georgia mutters, worry coloring her features. "Damn, I must have left my phone at the desk. I'll get it. How are you feeling? Should I call an ambulance? Yep, I should call an ambulance."

"No, no." I object, shaking my head a little too aggressively, which causes my vision to go hazy again. *Wow, I'm so light-headed.* "It's just a dizzy spell. I'm okay. I can finish . . ." I make a move to get up, and decide immediately that's not going to happen and sit back on the floor.

"Don't even think about moving just yet," Georgia says, her tone stern.

I nod, dropping my head into my hands. "You're right. I don't feel so great. I may need to go home."

"Okay, I'll drive you. Devon! DEVON!" Georgia shouts the owner's name until he rushes over, his expression panicked.

"What is it? What happened?" Devon gasps when he sees me. "Ana? You're so pale!"

"I think I need to go home," I manage to say, but Georgia cuts in.

"She collapsed mid-massage. I have no idea

what happened, but I'm going to drive her home and get her settled. Can you have Maggie take care of this super-understanding client while you watch the front desk?" She nods toward the woman on the table, who may be paler than me at this point. "Ana's appointments need to be rescheduled, and my next appointment too."

"Of course." Devon nods, frantic. "Please, go. Do you need anything before you leave, Ana? Mints? Orange juice?"

"There's orange juice here?" Georgia asks incredulously.

"In my personal fridge, yes."

Georgia exchanges a look with me, then shrugs. "Sure, we could use some orange juice."

Getting me off the floor and out the door isn't exactly easy.

"Well, if I knew passing out would get me special access to Devon's personal fridge, I would have done that ages ago," Georgia mutters.

I snicker, then wince. Each step makes my head spin like a dang windmill. It takes a bit, but Georgia helps me into her car with a promise to retrieve my car later today.

"Okay, what the fuck was that?" she asks once we're pulling out of the parking lot. "You scared the shit out of me."

"I'm sorry," I say, taking the tiniest sip of orange juice from the bottle. "I think maybe I just didn't eat enough this morning."

"What did you eat?"

"Oatmeal. A banana."

"That seems like enough," she says, and she's right.

"I don't know what it is." I squeeze my eyes closed, willing myself not to barf in Georgia's car. The same car that she so kindly used to help move my things just days ago. *I can't puke.*

She must sense my stress because her tone changes drastically.

"That's okay," she says, her voice soothing. "Just give me the address of your friend's place, and I'll take you there and get you settled. Will your friend be home? I don't think you should be left on your own."

"His name is Grant," I mumble, resting my forehead against the cool glass of the passenger side window. "He's on the hockey team, and I'm pretty sure he'll be training."

Georgia gasps. "Like, *the* hockey team? Wow, okay, I wasn't expecting that, but I'm rollin' with it."

I haven't told her that I'm staying with one of Jason's teammates. I guess I was worried that would make me sound like some kind of slut, jumping from bed to bed, but Georgia doesn't seem to be judging me. She just seems surprised.

I guess I am too. I never would have imagined how sweet Grant could be.

When I give her the address, she punches it into her phone, and we're off. Only ten more minutes of my brain and stomach battling at who can spin the fastest before I'm tucked safely into bed.

When I unlock the door to the condo, Georgia close behind me, I expect Hobbes to run to the door. What I don't expect is for Grant to follow. Hobbes scampers up to me, jumping and barking with pure elation that I've come home unexpectedly.

Grant steps into the hall, a plate of toast in his hands. He's wearing athletic track pants that stretch around his muscular thighs and a T-shirt that accentuates his bulky chest and arms. I would laugh at the look of surprise on his face if I weren't so terrified of puking on his nice wood floor.

"Hey," he says as he approaches, his brow furrowed. "Everything okay?"

"Oh, wow. *Hello*." Georgia giggles with a small wave, and I roll my eyes.

Not the time.

"I'm just not feeling well," I say with a grimace.

Before I can continue, Grant's hands are on my shoulders, his torso bent over to align our faces. He brushes his fingers against my cheek, and I involuntarily lean into the cool touch.

"You're really flushed."

"Well, I was pale before, so that's good?"

"Let's get you in bed. It's down the hall, third door on the left," he tells Georgia, who gently guides me in that direction. "I'll grab some water and a cool cloth."

"You didn't tell me your friend was *smokin' hot*," she whispers in my ear, and I snort.

"Hard to bring up in conversation." I sigh, but a smile twitches my lips. *Glad she agrees.*

"Um, not *that* hard," Georgia says. She helps me under the covers with a promise to bring me a cup of tea in, and I quote, "Tea minus three minutes." After sliding the small trash can over to my bedside, *just in case*, she scurries off to the kitchen.

I can vaguely make out the sounds of Georgia's pleasant voice introducing herself to Grant, followed by his deep baritone. Guess you can add "meet the friends" to the list of situations I'm not emotionally prepared for. Not that Grant and I are . . . *Never mind.*

Georgia comes back in the room moments later with a cup of steaming tea in her hands. "Here you go, some nice Mint Medley. He's got a decent stash of tea for a dude."

"I bought the tea," I say with a small smirk, accepting the cup.

She nods. "Ah, that makes more sense."

I blow on the tea, still a little too hot to sip. Georgia watches me with x-ray vision eyes.

"I'm really okay," I tell her.

"Are you sure?" she asks, glancing at her phone.

"I'm sure. I still have no idea why I passed out

like that."

She gives me a sad little nod. "You just stay in bed and rest. As for me . . . I guess I could still go back to work. I've got a few appointments later today. And the tips these folks give are always—" She pauses, bringing her thumb and forefinger together into an A-OK sign with a wink.

"Please, go. You've done enough."

Debating, she bites her lip. Finally, she claps her hands together and stands.

"Okay, if you insist. But you must know, I'm only leaving because you're clearly in good hands." She winks. "Good, strong hands." She winks again. "Good, strong, sexy hands."

"Stop," I say on a groan, but I can't hide my chuckle.

"Good, strong, sexy, *large*—"

"Good-bye, Georgia!" I say louder than necessary.

She blows me a kiss on her way out the door. I listen to her say some lengthy good-byes to Grant, likely threatening him with promises to call the police and accuse him of kidnapping me if he doesn't take good care of me. Just normal friend stuff.

I hum a contented smile, my dizziness finally slowing to a faint spin. I take a small sip of tea. It's still a little too hot but the mint is calming, so I take another sip. Once all the tea has hit my belly and my legs and fingers feel warm again, I snuggle under the covers.

What a weird day.

I close my eyes, which proves to be a mistake. The room spins again, the blackness behind my closed eyes only making me feel more untethered. My stomach lurches, and I know I have about ten seconds before all that minty goodness comes rushing up again.

I throw off the duvet and rush to the bedroom door, swinging it open with what little energy I have. I bolt across the hall past Grant, who slams his body against the wall to make room. I'm barely bent over the toilet before the tea, orange juice, oatmeal, and God knows what else comes out of me. I try not to think too hard about it. Instead, I take slow breaths, steadying my breathing as tears sting my eyes. *I hate throwing up. Hate, hate, hate it.*

I hear the door creak open through my panting.

"Can I come in?" Grant's soft, soothing voice says from behind me.

I nod in response, coughing once before flushing the toilet.

Somehow, Grant seeing me at my worst doesn't bother me as much as I thought it might. Maybe because of that day he rescued me from my apartment, broken and bloody. Maybe because he's always so strong and composed—nothing seems to bother the guy.

He holds out a glass of water, a thermometer, and a damp washcloth.

"Thank you." I swish my mouth with the room-temperature water and spit. Leaning back against the side of the tub with a groan, I stick the thermometer in my mouth. *It must be the stomach flu.*

While we wait for the thermometer to give us the verdict, Grant presses the cool washcloth to my cheek. His touch is soft and methodical, his eyes revealing equal parts concern and concentration. My pulse has slowed to a regular rhythm when the thermometer beeps. Grant pulls it from my mouth, squinting at the numbers.

"What's it say?"

"You don't have a fever. Could it be food poisoning?"

I shake my head. "I've had food poisoning before. This isn't that bad."

"Then what is it?" Grant frowns, confusion in his voice.

I sigh, going back over the list of what I've eaten lately, where I could have caught something, when I last felt so crummy . . .

Oh no.

"What day is it?"

"Tuesday. Coach gave us the day off."

"No, I mean, what's the date?"

He thinks it over for a second. "The eighteenth. Why?"

A cold shock slithers down my spine. With all the changes in my life lately, I haven't been paying as close attention as I should have. *I'm late.* I lift a shaking hand to my mouth.

"What's the matter? Ana?" Grant lifts my chin with his fingers.

Oh God. I meet his eyes. "I need to go to a drugstore."

"You can't go like this. I'll go. What do you

need?"

I wish I could flush myself down the toilet and disappear like my breakfast.

My voice is low and timid when I reply. "A pregnancy test."

Grant nods slowly. I can see him processing this information, his jaw clenching and unclenching. We're silent for a moment, our eyes locked and mouths shut.

Suddenly, he stands, running a hand through his hair. "I'll get one delivered."

"You can't get them delivered. They aren't like pizzas."

Oh fuck. The thought of pizza—cheesy, gooey, sloppy pizza—sends another wave of nausea shooting from my belly to my throat.

I push Grant out of the way and hang my head over the toilet again. I feel like I'm dying, emptying my insides like this. The only thing keeping me grounded is Grant's hand on my back, rubbing in soothing circles.

"You're okay," he murmurs when I lift my head with a sob.

We repeat the process again—me swishing water and cleaning my mouth, and him wiping my face with a cool cloth.

"I'm going to pick you up, okay?"

I nod.

Grant lifts me in one gentle motion, not too quickly, but steady. I nestle my head against his shoulder, curling into the warmth radiating from beneath his thin T-shirt. He carries me across the hall into his room, saying something about the blackout blinds being better, and I'm too tired to argue. He settles both of us gently on the bed. I sink back into him, willing whatever is left in my stomach to settle.

"I'm so sorry," I mutter, hating myself for being such a burden.

"Don't be sorry." He breathes into my hair, one hand seeking mine. "Just rest."

As our fingers curl together, I let my eyes close. I don't realize it at first, but our breathing falls into a steady pace, matching in perfect time.

I feel so secure in Grant's arms, more than I have ever in my life. With my fingers clasped with his, I drift away.

● ● ●

My dreams are interrupted by barking, and then voices. The deep rasp of male voices.

"Two bottles of Gatorade. Two tests—early-detection kind. Some of those Pepto tablets, and some carbonated water."

I'm trying to make sense of the strange list before I open my eyes and register where I am. I reach across the duvet, squinting at the rosy light spilling in through the curtains. It has to be late afternoon already.

The door is half-open, two voices carrying clearly from the hall. It's Grant and . . . Jordie? Yes, that sounds just like Jordan Prescott, twenty-five-year-old hotshot left winger, a.k.a. a rookie on the team. I've always been a little aware of Jordie, since Jason was constantly threatened by his mere existence. Not to mention that the guy is really talented on the ice. And totally cute too.

Feeling much better than I did before I fell asleep, I slip out of bed. Wrapping myself in an oversized cardigan, I tiptoe down the hall and find I was right. Jordie stands across from Grant, whose broad back is to me.

One by one, Jordie pulls items out of a brown paper bag and sets them on the kitchen counter. "Saltine crackers, chicken noodle soup, some orange juice—"

"You can keep the orange juice. She's not going to want that. Lost a ton already."

"Shit, really?"

"Yeah. Thanks for all of this, Jordie. I owe you one, big time." Grant claps Jordie on the back, who looks up at him and grins.

"Nah, man. We're good. You would have done the same thing for me. No questions asked."

I hate to interrupt this moment between friends, but the men haven't noticed me yet. I clear my throat and wave at Jordie, whose eyes practically bug out of his head.

"A-Ana?"

"Hi, Jordie."

"Oh," Jordie chokes out. "I didn't know . . . this stuff is for *you*?"

Interesting. So Grant had him run an errand, but didn't mention who the woman in question was who needed these things.

Grant approaches me with a concerned expression. "Are you okay?"

I return his look with a reassuring smile. "I feel so much better now. Thank you."

"Did you sleep?" he asks in a soft voice.

I nod.

"Okay," Grant says, but his eyes tell me he isn't entirely convinced.

I don't blame him. I'm known for making a molehill out of a mountain. I'd downplay getting shot if I had to.

"So," Jordie says, pointing at the supplies emptied out onto the counter, to me, to Grant, and back at me. "Are you two . . ."

Oh Jesus.

Grant steps between us, entirely blocking my view of Jordie with his massive body. "Friends. Besides that, you don't know a goddamn thing."

"Understood."

"I'm dead serious, Jordie. If you breathe a word of this to anyone . . ."

"I wouldn't."

Placing one hand on Grant's back to calm him, I peek around his torso to catch Jordie's eye. "Thanks, Jordie."

"Just following orders, ma'am." He grins with a boyish twinkle in his eye.

"I'll walk you out," Grant mutters, nudging his teammate on the shoulder and turning him toward the door.

Jordie calls over Grant's wall-like shoulder with some effort. "Maybe it's just the flu! Feel better, Ana."

"Hope so! Thanks."

Grant and Jordie stand in the doorway for a moment, their voices low and almost indiscernible. I hear the name *Kress* and suddenly realize I don't need to hear this conversation.

I step over to the counter, covered in an assortment of items you might receive in a care package. I smile, unscrewing the top of a blue sports drink, and take a tentative sip. When my stomach doesn't flip-flop all over the place, I take a full swig, appreciating the feel of sugar hitting my bloodstream again.

Then, before I can think too hard about it, I

pick up both of the pregnancy tests and head to the bathroom. After selecting one, I tear the box open and read the directions, pull my yoga pants down, and sit on the toilet. Now would be the moment to utter a prayer, but I'm not sure what I would ask for. I'm not ready to have a . . . *baby*. I can barely *think* the word, let alone speak it.

When I'm done, I set the stick on the edge of the sink and wait. No use panicking. It'll be whatever it's going to be. Until then . . .

Deep breaths.

CHAPTER SIXTEEN

Consequences

Grant

Deep breaths.

Ana closed herself inside my bathroom with the pregnancy tests five minutes ago, and I'm practically vibrating with anxiety while I wait for her to come out. With absolutely zero chill, I pace the hallway, running through various scenarios in my mind while nervous energy swims inside me.

Hobbes, sensing something is up, scratches at the floor near my feet and looks up at me.

"What?" I say, agitated.

He yips out a reply and dances around.

With a sigh, I bend down and lift him with one hand under his belly. Stalking over to the bathroom door, I give it a gentle knock. "Hey, Ana?"

"Be out in a minute." Her voice is muffled through the door, and I can't tell if she's upset, or relieved, or something in between.

"I'm just going to take Hobbes out. Take your time."

I secure his leash to his collar and head out. "You've got shit timing, you know that?"

He looks up at me with brown eyes and licks his nose. Then again, maybe taking Hobbes outside is better than standing around waiting for news I'm not even sure I'm ready to hear.

As Hobbes squats and pees on the grass, I can't help the thoughts swirling inside my head. Thoughts about the night of the storm when I came home and found Ana in my bed . . . and more specifically, what happened after.

I was bare that night. We were so caught up in the moment, we didn't even stop to think.

Well, that's not true. A split second before I came, it did cross my mind, but I was already there, erupting inside her like half a second later. I figured she was on the pill. Stupid of me, I know.

Still, I don't regret what we did. That night was one of the best I've had in a very long time. A sweet woman in my bed, begging me to hold her and make her feel good? I felt useful. Needed. I was on top of the world that night.

But actions have consequences, and those consequences might be that we're going to have a baby. Maybe that should scare me, but if anything, it only makes me feel more for Ana. It makes me want to protect her and take care of her.

God, seeing her sick today, hunched over the toilet? I felt so helpless. I just wanted to fix it.

By the time I make it back inside, Ana's sitting on the couch, facing away from me. Her shoulders rise with a deep breath, and when Hobbes barrels over to her, she murmurs something soft to him, ruffling his fur with her fingers.

My throat is bone dry. I take a step closer to the couch, then pause and run one hand along the stubble on my jaw. "So, uh, how are you feeling?"

She licks her lips and meets my eyes. "Maybe you'd better sit down." Her eyes are red and look like she's been crying.

My chest tightens.

Following her instructions, I sit in the chair across from her. "Everything okay?"

She nods and swallows hard. She's hesitating. Like she's afraid I'll freak out at the news.

"Whatever it is, you can tell me. Whatever happens, I promise I can handle it." My voice is soft, deep, and sincere.

"I'm pregnant."

"Pregnant," I repeat softly.

She nods again.

"How are you feeling?" I move closer to sit beside her on the couch.

She inhales and lifts one shoulder. "Still a little nauseated, but okay."

"I meant about the news. That's big, right?"

Ana and I have covered a lot of topics in the short time she's been staying here, but she's never mentioned if she wants children or not. She'd make an amazing mother, I'm sure of it, but I don't know if this is what she saw in her future plans.

"A lot of things. It's hard to put into words."

I nod. "I'll bet."

She gives me a weak smile. "I feel . . . overwhelmed. In disbelief." She exhales slowly. "And so incredibly *embarrassed*."

"Why embarrassed?"

She twists her hands in her lap, and I can practically see the discomfort rolling off her in waves. "Well, because I don't know if the baby is yours or Jason's."

My stomach tightens, and I release a slow exhale. "Yeah. I was wondering about that too."

"I feel so stupid." She drops her face into her hands and lets out a deep groan. "Or maybe slutty is a better word."

"Hey." Squeezing her shoulder, I move closer. "Don't ever call yourself that."

Ana scoffs. "Well, what kind of woman doesn't know who the father of her baby is?"

With a soft touch to her cheek, I turn her face toward mine. "The kind who ended one relationship and moved on with her life. There's nothing wrong with what we did, Ana."

For the first time, I realize I actually believe those words. I felt guilty at first—because as a teammate's ex, she should have been off-limits to me. But somewhere along the way, those feelings went away. Maybe because I'd have to respect

Kress in order to feel guilty about sleeping with his girl. And I definitely don't respect him.

"Then why did you say it couldn't happen again?" she asks, pinning me with a serious stare.

Jesus. What does one say to that?

Because it would be so easy to fall for you? Because I would never be okay being your casual fuck buddy? Because you're the kind of girl who makes a guy want it all—a white picket fence, kids in the backyard, a dog who's a total pain in the ass but you love anyway.

I force my gaze to return to hers. "Because I didn't think you'd be ready to jump into another relationship."

She chews on her lower lip, still watching me. I'm wondering if she's going to point out that people don't have to be in a relationship to fuck, but she doesn't. *Thank God.* She just stays quiet with an emotion I can't read written all over her face.

I'm not the type who can separate sex from feelings. Maybe it's because I've been alone for too long. Maybe because some part of me has already fallen for her. Who the hell knows?

When Ana doesn't say anything else, I touch

her hand. "It's going to be okay."

She looks uncertain. "Are you sure?"

"Very."

If the baby's mine, I have enough money and resources to make sure both her life, and our baby's, is comfortable and safe. And even if the baby's not mine, hell, that doesn't change much in my eyes, because my number one priority now is ensuring that both Ana and the baby are safe.

"You can stay here as long as you like. I'll do whatever I can to protect you both. And if it's mine, well . . ."

She looks up, her delicate eyebrows arched, waiting for the next words out of my mouth.

"I've always wanted kids. A whole bunch of them."

She smiles, her face relaxing. "But I'm guessing you didn't imagine it would be like this."

"I didn't, but that doesn't change anything. If the baby's mine, I'll do everything in my power to make sure you're both happy and healthy. And if it's not, I'm still going to be here. This is *your* baby, Ana, and I'll protect you both."

"Grant . . ." Tears well in her eyes and she looks down at Hobbes, not wanting me to see her cry.

"We'll just face one thing at a time."

She shifts on the cushion, tucking her hair behind one ear. "Okay." Her voice is small and raspy with emotion.

"Let's feed you two. Think you can handle dinner?"

She nods, a soft smile on her face at the mention of feeding both her and the baby. "I'm starved, actually."

"Good. Something bland and easy on your stomach, or . . ."

"Enchiladas from Casa Mana." She grins, her eyes lighting up. "With extra jalapeños."

"Or that," I say with a chuckle.

"And maybe a movie. A comedy."

Rising to my feet, I can't help the smile on my face. "I'll order dinner. You can pick the movie."

Ana lets out a happy sound. It's just a sigh, really, but I can tell she's starting to believe that maybe everything really will be okay.

Somehow.

Maybe.

I hope.

CHAPTER SEVENTEEN

Going Home

Ana

Waking up in my childhood bed is a strange enough experience. But hearing the distant clatter of my father down the hall, starting the morning coffee? It's almost like I've gone back in time.

Actually, I've come home, but only for a few days. I got in late last night and surprised my father. The look on his face when he answered the doorbell to find me on the stoop was sweeter than any pastry I could whip up.

I check my phone. Almost eight a.m. I wonder if Grant's already at practice.

Reminding myself that I don't need to be thinking about Grant right now, I toss my phone aside. I snuggle briefly under the worn covers, willing myself back to a time when boy troubles only went as far as Corey Sullivan in the tenth grade. To a time before I found out I was pregnant.

But coffee lures me out of bed, like it has every day since I started drinking it. And since I'm still allowed one cup a day now that I'm pregnant, that's exactly what I'll have. I pull my tangled hair into a low ponytail, then slip off my pajama pants and oversized T-shirt to step into some jeans and a sweater.

In the kitchen, my dad is standing over the stove, flipping what I assume are pancakes, based on the slight burnt smell.

"Good morning," I call over the hiss of the batter in the pan.

"Ana! Help me out with this." He waves the spatula in the air. "I haven't made pancakes in years. It's like riding a bicycle. Gotta run into a few trees first."

"What's the occasion?" I smile, plucking the spatula from his hand and then removing the pancakes from the pan. *He forgot to add cooking spray.*

"You're home." Dad chuckles. "That's an occasion for me."

I pause my rummaging through the cabinets in my search for something to grease the pan, and turn to give my father an apologetic frown. I know how distant I've been the past few years. I'd blame it entirely on Jason, but that wouldn't be the whole story.

"I'm sorry, Dad," I say, taking a step toward him. "I felt like I had to do everything myself, you know? I just wanted to be independent."

"I suppose I taught you that," he grumbles, but he's smiling, so I'll call that a win. "C'mere."

My dad pulls me into a bear hug and squeezes me so hard, for a second, I can't breathe.

"Sorry." He grins when he releases me. "I missed you."

"I missed you too," I say softly, reaching up to gently squeeze his shoulder. "Now, let me get back to the pancake crisis over here, and then we can sit down and catch up."

• • •

"You're sure?"

I nod, biting my lip.

My dad's array of reactions to the story of Jason's misdeeds varied. Anger, to sadness, and finally to a deep disdain. But now that I've told him about the little human growing inside me? His expression is unreadable.

This is exactly why I haven't been telling people. Even after I knew, and half the hockey wives and fiancées kept calling to express their support after the video of Jason and me leaked, I couldn't bring myself to tell anyone the rest of my news. I just accepted their support and stayed quiet about my pregnancy, like maybe if I didn't say it out loud, I wouldn't have to deal with all this yet. Because the truth is, I have no idea how to deal with it.

Sadly, I know that's not the way this works. Ready or not, I'm going to have a baby.

"I took two pregnancy tests. I was thinking about visiting Dr. Hao while I'm here, if she has any openings."

Dr. Hao was my mother's ob-gyn, and mine. Well, during high school and before I moved away.

"I can call her. I saw her at the rally a few months ago, and we chatted."

My heart swells three times its normal size. First, because my father is still participating in our town's awareness campaigns for drunk driving.

For my mom. And second, because my father had a conversation with an attractive woman, something he couldn't do for years after Mom passed. And third? Because I can't find a hint of anger in his voice about my pregnancy news.

"You're not mad?" I ask tentatively.

Dad reaches across the table, taking my small, smooth hand in his big, scratchy one. "Ana. I couldn't be mad. I'm so proud of you. Proud that you left that piece-of-crap ex of yours. Proud that you're taking care of yourself. Proud that you're going to be just as excellent a mother as your mom was. And proud that you're making me a granddaddy and giving me another human to love unconditionally."

The tears well up in my eyes so fast, I have to blink them away to see clearly.

"Thank you, Daddy," I whisper, so grateful to the universe for putting such a kind, sensitive, loving soul in my life. "You don't know how much that means to me. You're going to be the best granddaddy ever."

• • •

At my appointment the next day, Dr. Hao confirms

that I am indeed pregnant, which comes as no surprise. Dad comes back in the room and squeezes my hand at the news. When the appointment over, I promise Dr. Hao that I'll find an obstetrician and schedule an ultrasound when I return to Seattle, and Dad promises her that they'll go get coffee soon and catch up.

Back at home, I head into my room while Dad makes himself busy with a crossword puzzle. I pick up my phone and call the first person I think of.

"Hey, babe! How'd it go?" Georgia chirps on the other end.

"Good, I guess. The doctor said everything seems normal."

"Oh, that's a relief. This whole thing is crazy. How are you even pregnant?"

"Well . . ." I want to crack a joke about the birds and the bees, but I'm feeling uninspired. *I can only joke to a certain extent when my reality is . . . this.*

"I just can't believe you're going to have a baby," Georgia says, her voice almost a little sad.

My chest clenches painfully. Will things change between us once there's a kid involved?

"I know, me neither." I close my eyes tightly,

praying that our friendship won't be affected by my new reality.

"Well, thanks for calling, babe. Keep me updated, okay?"

I sigh, a little relieved, and also a little surprised that she's cutting the call so short. But she seemed interested, so she's still invested, and that feels like a good sign to me.

"Of course."

We say our good-byes and I roll over on the bed, scrolling for the next contact on my list.

"Hey," Grant says, his voice rumbling pleasantly in my ear.

"Hi there," I say, pretending not to notice the way my heart skips a beat when he speaks.

"What did the doctor say?"

Ah, straight to business.

"That I'm definitely pregnant. And everything looks fine."

"What do you mean, everything? You and the baby?"

"Apparently, yes."

"Good." Grant lets out a sigh.

His relief is contagious, so I lean back against the pillows stacked on my bed and smile.

"How are you feeling?" he asks after a moment.

"I'm okay," I say firmly. He spends way too much time worrying about me. But I would be lying if I said I didn't enjoy the attention sometimes.

"You sure? No dizziness or anything? Nausea?"

"I'm sure. I feel so much better than I did the other day. I'm even holding down my dad's pancakes."

"That's good to hear. And how is your dad? With everything?"

I chuckle, suddenly imagining a meeting between my dad and Grant. Talk about worrywarts.

"He's being very supportive. I told him all about Jason too. About the breakup, anyway."

"Oh?" There's a hint of something in Grant's voice, but I can't make it out.

"Yes. He, um, thinks the baby is Jason's. And I didn't tell him otherwise," I say carefully.

"Right, makes sense," Grant says on the other

end, and I can imagine him nodding solemnly like he does whenever he has something more to say.

"My dad wants to kill him," I find myself saying, unsure why I'm sharing this. "I'm pretty sure he wants to hunt him down and make him suffer."

"He's not the only one."

I roll my eyes. *Men.*

"Have you told him yet?" Grant asks.

"Jason?"

"Yeah."

"Not yet. But I need to, soon. It's the right thing to do." I scratch at a spot behind my knee. I'd rather never talk to Jason again, but he needs to know that I could potentially be carrying his baby.

"I guess so."

I frown. Grant clearly has something else to say, but as always, he's self-censoring. I'd be aggravated if I weren't so sure that he's putting my feelings first.

"So, you're getting enough to eat?"

I grin. "I'm fine. I promise."

"When are you coming home?" Grant asks next.

I think we're both surprised by the use of the word *home* to describe Grant's condo, because a silence falls over the call.

"Uh, well . . ." I stammer, eager to banish any awkwardness. He could just be talking about Seattle in general. "Probably the day after tomorrow. I don't work again until later this week."

"All right, well, let me know. I can pick up some groceries, and we'll have dinner."

I chew on my lip. When are you going to stop using Grant, Ana?

"Sounds good," I say, feigning enthusiasm. *It's just dinner.*

"I'll talk to you later."

"You bet. 'Bye, Grant."

"'Bye, Ana."

I hang up, tossing my phone on the bed beside me and closing my eyes for a moment. The sigh that comes out of me is tired and weak.

How nice would it be to simply rest in the assurance that Grant will take care of me? I touch my belly. *Of us?*

But I know myself, and I know I can't let him put aside everything to do that. I can't derail his entire life just because mine is messed up.

I won't.

CHAPTER EIGHTEEN

Unexpected Action

Grant

The ballroom is decked out in elaborate bunches of sunny yellow balloons that arch over doorways, and huge bouquets of yellow roses in the center of each round table. Tonight's gala is meant to raise money for a domestic violence safe house here in Seattle, and it looks like the turnout is great.

Coach Dodd thumps me on the shoulder as I pass, giving me a thumbs-up, but I don't pause to talk with him. I weave my way through the crowd, scanning for Ana.

She may be staying at my place, but I haven't seen much of her since she returned from visiting her Dad last week. A midweek trip to the Northeast kept me away, and this week I spent several days in Canada for a series of away games. I've been looking forward to the chance to see her tonight, eager to check on her and find out how she's been feeling.

I had to be here two hours early for a photo shoot, which meant even though Ana agreed to come as my date tonight, we didn't arrive together. And I'm starting to get a little itchy in this tuxedo, because the party started twenty minutes ago and I still haven't seen her.

Reaching into my jacket pocket for my phone, I check the time again and note I don't have any missed calls or texts from her.

"Grant, over here!" I hear Jordie call from across the room.

I follow the sound of his voice and spot him standing beside a table filled with my teammates and their wives and girlfriends.

When I get closer, I realize Ana is there too, and for a moment, my size thirteen feet stop working.

God, she looks beautiful.

I can't help my gaze from wandering the length of her, or the way it lingers over her stomach, which is still flat. Her golden hair is down tonight and has been straightened, lying in a silky sheet over each of her shoulders. Her brown eyes are lined with mascara and that other stuff, eyeliner maybe? A simple black sheath dress that falls to her knees and a pair of black heels complete her look. She looks classy. Sophisticated. Beautiful.

Her gaze meets mine, and my breath catches. Then a smile slowly spreads across her face.

"Grant," she murmurs, lifting on her toes when I bend down to hug her.

"Damn. You look gorgeous."

She chuckles, patting the lapel of my jacket. "You clean up nice too. Did you shave?"

I grin, running one hand along my jaw. "Yeah. I figured it was time."

She leans in a little closer. "I'm not sure what I like best. Scruff or no scruff."

Jordie watches our interaction with an amused expression. But thankfully, everyone else seems too engrossed in their own conversations to notice me basically losing my shit over how gorgeous this girl is.

"Who wants wine?" Elise, the fiancée of my best center, holds up two bottles.

Jordie hands me a glass, and I hold it out, accepting a pour of red wine.

Elise holds up the bottles. "Ana, red or white?"

Ana makes a face, and I can tell she's debating whether to tell everyone she's pregnant. It's early still. From what I read, women don't usually begin sharing the news they're pregnant until later in the first trimester. Something about the chance of miscarriage being higher. There's a lot of scary shit I read, to be honest.

"Ana?" Elise asks with wide, eager eyes.

Ana smiles demurely, still thinking it over. "Surprise!" She lets out an uneasy laugh. "I'm expecting. Which I realize is a little, well, *unexpected*, but . . ." She shrugs. "Yeah."

My teammate Owen's wife, Becca, who is also pregnant, takes Ana's hand and squeezes. "This is amazing news. Everything happens for a reason."

Ana nods. "True. It was a bit shocking at first, but I'm excited."

"How far along are you?" Elise asks.

"When are you due?" Becca says next.

"Just six weeks, and um, mid-June." Ana's

cheeks are pink as she answers these, and other questions, like about how she's feeling and what she thinks about natural childbirth, and if she plans to breastfeed.

It's a lot. Based on Ana's surprised reaction, I'm not even sure that she knows the answers to some of these questions yet. I love my teammates, but their wives can be a bit much.

Exchanging an uneasy look with Owen and Justin, I shove one hand in my pocket. They have no reason to suspect the baby could be mine. And since now is not the time, I decide not to bring it up.

I lean in close while the excited chatter continues around Ana. "Can I get you something to drink?" I ask her in a low voice, hoping to save her from any further embarrassment.

She flashes me a grateful look. "Grapefruit juice?"

"Of course." I make my way over to the bar and place her order.

"Sorry, sir, we don't have grapefruit juice. We have orange, pineapple, or cranberry."

"Thanks anyway." On the way back to the table, I intercept a busboy, stopping him with a stern look. "Hey, kid, can you do me a favor?"

His eyes widen. "You're Grant Henry."

I nod, fishing my wallet out of my back pocket. "Run to the corner market, and this is yours." I flash him a crisp hundred-dollar bill.

"Uh, sure," he says, nodding. "What did you need?"

"Grapefruit juice. Bring it directly to me. I'll be over there." I point toward the table where Ana is now sitting between Elise and Becca, nodding along to something one of them is saying.

The busboy dashes away, and I rejoin my friends at the table. Ana's too immersed in the conversation to notice that I've returned without her beverage. But less than five minutes later, the busboy comes through.

"Thanks, man," I say, tipping him.

"Can I, uh, get your autograph?" he asks, handing me the bottle of juice.

"Sure." I scrawl out a quick signature on the back of the receipt and hand it to him.

Jordie gives me a strange look as the guy saunters away, but I ignore it. Twisting off the top of the glass bottle, I pour Ana's grapefruit juice into a glass and hand it to her.

She pauses in the middle of her conversation about breast versus bottle feeding and gives me an appreciative look. "Thank you."

"Anytime," I murmur.

Ana takes a sip and makes a little pleasure-filled sound that I feel down in my balls.

Awesome.

Unease tightens inside my chest. I'm going to need something stronger than wine. I don't know how it's *not* obvious to everyone at this table the attraction I feel toward Ana. Hell, maybe it is, and I'm terrible at faking.

"Jordie, what are you drinking?" I ask, tipping my chin toward the bar.

"I'll walk with you," he says.

Out of earshot of the rest of our friends, he wastes no time digging in. "So, you and Ana?" he asks as we pause beside the bar, waiting our turn to be served.

I give him a blank look, hoping my lack of enthusiasm for this topic will be a clear signal. Sadly, Jordie is undeterred. His mouth twists in a wry grin. Clearly, he's enjoying my discomfort.

"When did this all happen?"

"Nothing's happening." My expression says to leave it alone, but of course Jordie's not going to do that.

"But . . ."

"Just drop it, Jordie." My tone is biting.

"Dude. You can't just shut me out. I have so many questions."

"Well, I don't have answers. So, like I said, drop it."

The bartender approaches, and Jordie orders a beer while I request a gin and tonic.

"Top shelf, if you have it," I say, sliding the bartender a large tip.

"Certainly, sir." He nods.

With our drinks in hand, we start back toward the table.

"But you don't date," Jordie says with a raised brow.

"We're not dating," I mutter without meeting his eyes. *Because she's not looking for a relationship*, my brain helpfully reminds me.

I know Jordie's had questions ever since that night he brought over the pregnancy tests. And now that Ana and I are here together, and she's just announced her pregnancy, it's only natural that he's asking. But I meant it when I told him I don't have any answers. Shit, his guess is as good as mine about what's happening between us.

I take a deep breath. "Listen, it's not going anywhere, okay? She's staying with me for a bit, that's it."

He makes an annoyed sound. "Whatever you need to tell yourself."

Now, I'm the one feeling annoyed. I don't need him giving me the third degree I about this, especially because I don't have any answers. "Besides I don't like dogs," I blurt out.

He smirks. "Uh huh."

"Fuck off Jordie. I'm serious."

He turns to face me, and his normally playful expression has been replaced by a somber one. "I saw the way you looked at her."

"Yeah, and how did I look at her?"

He meets my eyes. "Like you wanted to protect her. Take care of her."

Fuck. I guess I was more obvious than I thought. My Adam's apple bobs in my throat.

"I do. I am. It's the decent thing to do."

"I guess so." He nods.

We're almost back to the table and, thankfully, done with this conversation. I take a long swallow of my drink, hoping it will extinguish some of the anxiety stewing inside me.

CHAPTER NINETEEN

Sweet Relief

Ana

Part of me can't believe I'm here. Dressed in a little black dress, surrounded by Seattle's hockey elite and their plus-ones. I feel a little strange, like I'm invading a circle of friends I have no right to. Maybe it's because these are Jason's teammates, and their wives and fiancées. And since I'm no longer tied to Jason, I forfeited the right to be part of this group. But here they are, accepting me with kind smiles and warm hugs, and I'm grateful. I don't feel quite so alone.

When Grant asked me to attend as his date, I gave him a confused look. Then he stammered out something about driving separately, and I assumed he meant as friends. Still, I'm glad he invited me. The gala is being put on as a benefit for domestic violence—to provide aid for the women's shelter—and so, of course I wanted to come.

And while I totally didn't plan on telling anyone about my pregnancy tonight, I'm kind of relieved that I did. I'm glad that my big secret is out, especially because of how gracious they all were. Of course, I didn't miss the way some of Grant's teammates eyes had widened in shock, looking anywhere but directly at me. Awkward moment aside, the women were all supportive—asking me about a thousand questions I didn't have the answers to.

I guess I need to educate myself on a whole host of new topics, everything from birthing methods to vaccines to baby carriers. I had no idea becoming a mom would require an entire re-education. I figured I'd just wing it. Since Becca is pregnant too, a few months further along than I am, maybe I can lean on her for support. Lord knows I'll need it.

When Grant and Jordie venture over to the bar to order a drink, I can't help but notice their heads turned together, like they're discussing something serious in low tones. I wonder if *I'm* the topic of conversation. That thought sends a low buzz of awareness thrumming through me.

"So, what hospital are you going to deliver at?"

Becca asks, smiling sweetly at me.

"Oh, I'm not sure." I smile back.

She nods and launches into a *freaking TED talk* about the different choices of hospitals in this city. Clearly, she's done her research. I hear the word NICU and plan to Google it as soon as I get home.

As Becca chatters on, her humongous man candy of a husband stalks over and plants a kiss on the top of her head. She flashes him a sweet look and keeps right on talking.

When I'm ready to venture into the dating scene again, I'd love to have a stable, loving relationship like she's found with Owen. I know Becca had some trauma in her past. Know she was sexually assaulted, and that together, she and Owen had to work through a lot of her intimacy issues. Elise got drunk one time and overshared.

As I gaze at Becca, glowing with her pregnancy, I know she deserves all the good things in life. And I do too. It's just . . . I'm not in a place where I'm ready for them, if that makes sense.

I still have some healing I need to do. One thing at a time. I need to be happy on my own first, before I can give part of myself to another person. Maybe that sounds weird, but it's the truth.

But even if I'm not ready for something serious, I am grateful for Grant's presence in my life. Earlier, when he got me the drink I was craving—grapefruit juice—my heart squeezed inside my chest.

"Okay, enough baby talk," Elise says dramatically, raising her brows at Becca.

"Fine." Becca chuckles, flashing me an apologetic look. "I get carried away."

"No worries," I say with a smile.

My attention is grabbed by an older guy stopping at the table to talk to Grant. Grant rises from his chair and follows the man to the other side of the room, where he begins shaking hands and chatting with an older couple. I assume they're big donors for tonight's event, or something.

Elise's gaze follows Grant across the room too, and I'm kind of relieved, because it means I won't be caught ogling. He looks *damn good* in a classic black tuxedo. His hair is neatly combed and his defined jawline is clean-shaven without a trace of the dark stubble I've gotten used to.

"*Damn.* Grant *really* fills out that tux," she murmurs under her breath.

Becca and I both chuckle.

"Grant? Oh, he's hot as fuck," Sara says, finally joining the conversation now that it's no longer baby-dominated.

My gaze wanders the length of him. Powerful legs encased in his dress slacks. A tailored jacket that hugs his wide shoulders and arms before tapering at his trim waist. Adam's apple peeking out above his shirt collar. That full mouth that I've fantasized about kissing more than once . . .

"He'll definitely make some lucky girl very happy one day," Becca says with a nod.

Elise makes a noise of agreement. "I heard he doesn't date, though. Wonder why that is . . ."

Sara shrugs. "Not a clue. But it's a damn shame, because a body like that was built for riding."

The girls erupt into giggles as Sara's fiancé, Teddy, pauses beside us, making a *tsking* sound.

"Hey now," he says, scolding us, but his expression is playful.

The conversation moves on to another topic, but my gaze is still on Grant.

Grant. He's like a caramel—hard on the outside, and gooey on the inside. And I know how hot things get when he melts . . .

CHAPTER TWENTY

Going Deep

Grant

Tonight's gala has been a major success. I've schmoozed with donors, posed for selfies, and signed a few autographs, but I haven't spent much time with Ana, and it's time to rectify that. When Elise and Becca rise to go to the restroom, I reach down and pull Ana's chair closer to mine.

"Hey, you." I grin at her.

"Hey, stranger." She smiles back. Maybe it's her smile, or maybe it's the gin and tonic, but something inside me is feeling more at ease than before.

"Haven't seen much of you lately. How's Hobbes holding up? I'll bet he misses me."

She laughs. "Oh, he totally does. You should see him come five o'clock when you usually get home from the gym. He's beside himself when you don't come in."

I shake my head at the thought. Who knew I'd bond with her dog? "Everything else going okay? You haven't been getting sick anymore, have you?"

She shakes her head. "I've been feeling good. Just a little tired. Which I read is normal."

I nod. "I read that too. Your body needs the extra sleep. You're growing a human in there."

She sighs, a slight grin on her lips. "That's what they tell me."

"Did you get the vitamins I left for you?"

A smile overtakes her face. "I did. Thank you."

As she asks me about the trip to Canada, dinner is served. I fill her in on our two not-so-exciting losses as we eat chicken and potatoes and asparagus, and the rest of the team makes small talk. I'm pleased to see Ana eat every bite on her plate. She even helps herself to an extra roll from the bread basket.

The evening passes with a silent auction, dancing, and a whole lot of sexual tension. Actually, that last one might be just me. Because earlier, when Ana danced with me, I had a hard time keeping my body from reacting. But then she smiled when Jordie cut in, dancing with him with the same polite look she'd given me during our dance.

I might have told her that we couldn't be physical again, but right now, I'm feeling weak. If for some reason Ana decides she wants to get closer than dancing tonight, I'm not going to be strong enough to resist. I want her. And I really hope she wants that too.

When I take her hand again and nudge her toward the dance floor, she's laughing.

"I never took you for someone who likes to dance," she says, her brown eyes glittering at me.

I lift one shoulder. "Believe me, I'm not. You in this dress, though . . ." I give her a heated look. "Let's just say it's inspiring me."

She laughs. "Stop."

"If you like."

Her lips twitch.

She moves her hands up to my shoulders, and mine settle onto the dip in her waist. I put a couple of inches between us, needing a little distance so she doesn't feel my body's response to hers.

As we dance together in the center of the floor, I notice a few of my teammates watching us, but I don't care. Let them wonder. What's happening between Ana and me is no one else's business.

"Tonight's been fun," she says softly, her eyes moving from the three-piece band up to meet mine.

"It has." I nod. "I'm glad you came."

"Me too."

We continue swaying together while I fill Ana in on my upcoming travel schedule. Next week I'll be in Saint Louis and then Dallas, but this week I'm mostly home, except for a quick trip to California.

"Hobbes will be happy," she says, brushing a piece of lint from my shoulder.

"As important as Hobbes's happiness is to me, the reason I told you is just so you know you're more than welcome to stay there, even while I'm gone."

"Grant," she says sternly.

We've been over this. I really do want her to feel welcome.

"I'm serious. I'm gone at least three nights a week. Ana, I want you to stay. For as long as you want. I like knowing you and Hobbes will be there when I get home."

She softens, leaning in even closer. "I know. And you've been so incredible. I can't thank you enough."

"There's no need to thank me."

• • •

The rest of the evening passes in a blur, and then Ana and I are stepping out of a cab and riding the elevator up to my condo. Electricity still thrums steadily through my veins. It's like every moment has been swamped in anticipation, every look has been heated. I don't know if it's just me, or if Ana feels it too.

"I had a good time tonight," she says softly, moving inside the condo and setting her purse on the counter. Hobbes gives us a sleepy look from the couch where he's curled up, but doesn't move. "I guess I'd better go get out of this dress."

But when she turns to head down the hall, my fingers catch her elbow and I lightly tug. She turns, falling into my arms, and lifts her mouth to mine. And I can't resist for even a second longer.

Closing the distance between us, I press my lips

to hers. A surprised gasp escapes Ana as I deepen our kiss. She brings her hands beneath the lapels of my jacket to touch my chest, and for a second, I'm mentally preparing for her to push me away. But she doesn't, she just strokes the muscles in my chest and groans into my mouth.

I go from half hard to fully hard in an instant.

I held back at the gala, but now that she's in my arms, touching me, my self-control vanishes faster than a hockey puck into an empty net.

"What do you want?" she murmurs, her mouth busy kissing a hot path along my freshly shaven jaw.

"You."

It's only one word, but the effect on her is instantaneous. Her hands drop to my belt buckle, which she begins tugging at in an effort to free my erection. My cock presses painfully into my zipper.

"Bedroom," I choke out, panting, almost dizzy with need.

Ana's only taken two steps forward before I decide I'm too impatient to wait out the ten-second journey to my bedroom, and sweep her up in my arms instead. A breathless sound pushes past her lips the second I set her feet on the floor inside my bedroom. Two seconds later, she's stripped out of her dress and looking up at me with need-filled glittering eyes.

I brush my knuckles across the top of one of her breasts. "Take those panties off for me."

Ana complies, pushing her fingers into the sides of her thong until it slides down her hips so she can step out of the scrap of lace.

"On the bed. Let me look at you."

She crawls onto the bed, moving up toward my pillows and then lies back, her knees slightly parted.

Lust scrambles my brain as I move closer, leaning over her so I can kiss her sweet mouth again. Her tongue touches mine, and I groan, low in my throat. Using my thumb, I trace a slow circle around her clit while she squirms.

"Take these off," she murmurs, her fingers dragging down my zipper to free my cock.

While I shove my pants and boxers down and kick them off, Ana works on the buttons to my shirt. My jacket is somewhere on the floor. Then we're both naked and falling into the center of my bed together.

Ana's delicate fist curls around my cock, and she strokes it slowly. A wave of pleasure crashes through me.

"Grant," she says on a groan. She caresses my abs, and the muscles involuntarily clench at her touch.

"What do you want, baby?" *Baby?*

She doesn't so much as blink at the endearment. "You."

With pleasure.

I grab a condom from the drawer in my bedside table. I have no idea if we need one, or what possesses me—God knows she can't get *more* pregnant. But now doesn't seem like the time to have that conversation. And I want Ana to trust me, to know she can feel safe with me. So, condom it is. Every time. Until she tells me she wants it bare.

I suit up, and then I'm kneeling between her parted thighs, teasing her with the head of my dick. She shivers and presses her fingernails into my thigh.

"Tell me," I murmur, reaching down to pinch and tease her nipple. "What you want."

"Your cock."

I grip myself in one hand and ease in slowly. I've read that sex during pregnancy can be challenging, that she might feel sensitive from the extra hormones. So I move in slow, steady strokes, letting Ana dictate our pace.

"More," she says, whimpering, canting her hips up toward mine.

I don't want to be too rough with her, and force myself to keep my pace even, no matter how badly I want to drive hard and deep.

"Harder," she moans. "You're not going to break me."

With a rough caress, I hitch her thigh around my hip so I can drive in even deeper. She groans, and the sound hits me square in the chest.

My mouth finds her neck, and I leave hot, sucking kisses all over her skin. I'm trying to last, but I can't hold out much longer. She's reduced me to a trembling, groaning wall of pleasure.

"Need you to get there for me." I breathe hard, rubbing her clit with my thumb. My self-control is practically nonexistent.

Her body tightens around my shaft, and I groan.

A few more pumps and she comes apart, gripping me as she falls over the edge, pleasure ripping through her sweet body. Seconds later, I follow her, emptying myself in hot waves into the condom while I gather her close.

Afterward, I pull out slowly, missing the feel of her tight heat around me almost immediately.

I climb out of bed, naked and breathing hard, only long enough to deal with the condom and wash my hands. When I return, Ana's in the center of my bed, looking mighty comfortable.

I don't say a word as I slip in beside her and gather her close, until she's resting her head in the center of my chest. Her shaky breaths even out as we lie there together, and eventually my heart rate slows.

I may not know what I'm doing, but I know sex with her is incredible. The best I've ever had. I also know I feel things that go much deeper than friendship or mere obligation when it comes to her.

After a little while, I gather my courage and sit up. Ana does too, meeting my eyes.

She's still naked, and the sheet is down around her hips. And as beautiful as her breasts are, that's not the thing that catches my attention.

I can't help but notice her flat belly, the tiny knot of her belly button, and wonder how breathtaking she'll look with a round belly full of my baby. Knowing that the child inside her might not be mine sends all kinds of confusing feelings rushing through me.

"Grant? Do you want me to move to my own bed?" She tugs the sheet up to cover herself.

"No. I want you to stay." I touch her shoulder, brushing my calloused fingertips over her silky skin.

"Then what is it?"

I pause, running a hand over the stubble on my jaw. "No matter what happens, or how things turn out, I want a shot with you."

Her chin drops, and she exhales a big breath. I know what she's doing. She's preparing to let me down easy. The thought stings.

"Just say it, Ana." My tone comes out deeper than I intended, and she meets my eyes again.

"I'm sorry, but I can't jump into another relationship. I just need a friend right now."

A friend.

Her words are like a punch to the sternum, and there's a sudden ache in my chest that hurts worse than when I dislocated my shoulder last season.

Life has a pretty cruel sense of irony. I've spent my whole adult life single, and now I have a beautiful, kind, sweet woman in my bed who might be carrying my baby, and all she wants is to be my *friend*.

"Just get some sleep," I say, my throat tight, "and we can talk about it in the morning."

She nods and settles back into the pillows.

I cover her up with the duvet and lie down beside her, holding her close. But inside, I feel hollow and raw.

Love is that thing that people write poems and songs about. An elusive, magical feeling that's evaded me my entire adult life.

Now I've fallen headlong into it without my permission. And with a woman who doesn't want the same things.

CHAPTER TWENTY-ONE

Bump in the Road

Ana

I'm standing before the full-length mirror in Grant's bedroom when I hear Hobbes barking at the front door. There's a jangling of keys and then Grant walks in, home from running errands in under an hour.

His deep, familiar voice must be as soothing to Hobbes as it is to me, because the valiant little watchdog relents immediately. In the three months I've lived with Grant, they've really become besties. I can hear the jingle of Hobbes's collar as he inevitably rolls over to show Grant his fluffy belly. *Typical.*

Grant's soft murmurs carry pleasantly down the hall before he calls out to me. "I'm back!"

"Get over here!" I call back with a laugh. I can't wait to show him.

"What's up?" Grant says, stepping into his room with a furrowed brow. *Always concerned.*

"Stop worrying. It's a good thing."

I position myself in front of the mirror, standing sideways. Lowering the waistband of my yoga pants, I reveal the baby bump I've just discovered.

"Come here," I whisper, reaching out with one hand to pull Grant toward me. "Look."

"Is that . . ."

"The baby? Yes."

We're both staring at my belly in the mirror, a gleeful expression lighting up my features and an awestruck one on Grant's. I've officially *popped*, as the new-mommy blogs call it. They all assured me that this is one of the best parts. *I can see why.*

"I noticed that my pants were feeling a little tight, and voilà. I now have a baby bump."

"Incredible." Grant breathes out, his hands hanging at his sides.

Does he want to touch? I almost offer, but think better of it.

"I need to buy new clothes," I say quickly, pulling the waistband of my yoga pants back up. Uncomfortable, I wriggle a little. "Bigger clothes."

"I'll take you," he says.

I look up at him with a beaming smile. "Really?"

It's not that I love shopping. I'm just strangely excited to make the next moves in this new life of mine, even if those moves have a nasty price tag. Luckily, I've saved a little money . . . hopefully enough to buy a few pairs of maternity jeans and maybe a top or two.

"Really."

We eat a little lunch before we go, my mother's voice in my head insisting that I need to eat something before I go anywhere with a food court. But when we arrive at the mall, the scent of soft pretzels smothered in cinnamon sugar wafts across the court to my unsuspecting nose. *Oh, wow.*

"Shoot," I mumble, my stomach growling. I *just* ate. This is ridiculous.

"What's wrong?" Grant asks, using a soft touch to turn my shoulders so I'm looking at him.

"It's dumb," I say on a groan. "I'm just hungry

again."

"What do you want?"

"One of those dangerous cinnamon pretzels, but I'm stronger than my appetite," I say firmly, nodding with resolve. "Let me just distract myself with baby things, and I'll forget I want it."

I scurry into the nearest baby boutique, ignoring the fact that everything inside looks like it would punch a huge hole in this week's paycheck. I'm admiring a pair of tiny baby shoes with precious lacy ruffles when Grant finally joins me inside.

"Here you go," he says, holding out a paper bag with the pretzel company's logo winking at me from the side. "Eat it while it's hot."

My mouth waters as I blurt out a thank-you. I tear open the bag and inhale that sugary sweetness, savoring the scent before I demolish the pretzel in four bites. I try to be as dainty as possible, though, since Grant is watching.

"This is everything," I murmur between bites.

Grant chuckles, reaching out to smooth some hair off of my cheek and tuck it behind my ear. His eyes and his hand are both so warm, melting me with his sweet affection.

This man is going to be the death of me.

We walk around the mall for an hour, stopping in every store that promises a clearance section. Grant won't let me pay for a *single* thing. It's almost frustrating how chivalrous he can be. I decide not to make a big deal out of it, though. I know he's just trying to help. When I put an expensive lavender maternity dress back on the rack because the price made me pale, he steps aside to pay for it. I try not to notice.

With three bags full—the two largest in Grant's insistent hands—we call it quits. There's certainly more left to buy, but it can wait. On the walk back to the car through the parking garage, I realize that I'm rambling about cribs.

"I'm sorry." I laugh, tossing my bag into the trunk of Grant's car. "There's just so much left to buy. Maybe I need a rocking chair like the one my mom had. Or maybe I just want one. I don't know."

"Your mom used to rock you in a rocking chair?" he asks.

I nod, smiling. "Those are some of my earliest memories." As I say the words, I suddenly feel a little sad, because growing up in foster care, Grant probably doesn't have any of those early happy memories like I do. But he meets my eyes with a warm look.

"You sound excited," he says, his eyes flashing with something that looks like victory.

After spending so much time with the sad, weepy version of me, I'm sure this version is a treat. And I'm happy to keep her around as long as possible.

"I think I am." I sigh happily, watching Grant place his two bags in the trunk.

Together, we reach up and pull the door down, standing close once it locks in place. I smell his cologne, and I'm struck with vivid memories of the two times we slept together. The way his hands felt on my body . . . the way he moaned, deep and guttural, at my touch.

Easy, there. My heart rate picks up speed.

Grant leans against the car, looking at me with soft eyes.

"What?" I ask, curious to know what's on his mind.

"What if I got a three bedroom?"

"What do you mean?"

"We could keep things as they are. Me in my room, you in yours. And we'd still have room for a nursery. I know there are bigger units on other floors in my building."

"Grant . . ."

"Just think about it, okay?" He leans in, trying to catch my eyes with his magnetic gaze.

I automatically look at my shoes. I *do* think about it.

For a moment, I think about the allure of spending more time with Grant. How well he treats me. How wonderful he'd be with a baby. When my thoughts drift to the friendship I'd be jeopardizing, the way I'd feel relying on him for everything. I frown, meeting his eyes.

"I have thought about it, Grant. I need to get my own place before the baby comes."

He breaks eye contact with me then, staring over my head into the darkness of the garage. I can tell he's upset, but I don't know how to comfort him without sacrificing my own needs.

"I'm sorry," I say with a sigh. "I need to do this for myself. Do you understand?"

"I understand," he says, but all the buttery

warmth in his voice from today is gone.

He says he understands, but I'm not sure that he does. I need to stand on my own two feet. I'm going to be a mother, and taking care of *myself* seems like a pretty vital first step before I can take care of someone else.

"I'm tired, okay? Can we just go home?" I ask and then grimace, kicking myself for using the word *home* again. Of course the man is confused. I can't get my story straight.

"Sure."

And with that, Grant turns on his heel and walks around the car to the driver's side. I sigh and head to the other door.

Tension hanging in the air between us, we don't talk again for the entire ride home.

CHAPTER TWENTY-TWO

Baby Steps

Grant

Four months later

Earlier, when I got a text from Owen asking if I could come over and help him set up a bassinet for their new baby who arrived two weeks early, I jumped at the chance.

Things between Ana and me have been tense since she told me she wanted to move out before the baby is born and get her own place. She's been touring apartments with her friend Georgia in tow, rather than ask for my help. It's only a matter of time before she's gone, and even though I lived alone for a long time before Ana, I know this time, it'll be different. Quiet. And lonely.

When Owen opens the door to their penthouse

apartment, he's dressed in sweatpants and a green Ice Hawks T-shirt. His feet are bare, and his hair is rumpled in like eight different directions. I guess this is the look of new fatherhood. They've only been home from the hospital for three days.

"Hey, man. How's the family?"

He grins. "We're all doing good. But hey, thanks for coming. I couldn't handle another night of watching Becca cry when we put Bishop in his crib down the hall."

"Of course. It's no trouble."

I still can't believe they named their son Bishop after hockey goalie Ben Bishop. But then again, I guess it makes sense. The guy is one of Owen's personal heroes, and one of the best goaltenders in the league.

When Owen texted me asking for help, he only said they now wanted the baby to sleep in their room in a bassinet. He didn't mention the reason why. But now as we take the parts out of the box, he fills me in.

Apparently, the baby coming early changed how Becca felt about him sleeping in his crib in the nursery. She's been unexpectedly emotional and wants him close, sleeping in a bassinet beside their bed—at least while she's nursing him so frequently in the middle of the night.

I gather all of this from the few minutes of conversation Owen and I exchange before getting to work. I remove all the nuts and bolts from their packaging while he sets out the larger pieces of the bassinet—the cradle and the curved wooden legs it glides on. I wonder if Ana will change her mind on things after the baby comes. Things like wanting me closer? It's probably a long shot.

We work in relative silence for a while, making occasional small talk about the team.

An hour later, we're finished, and the final product looks pretty damn cute. I wonder if Ana will want one of these things to have the baby close to her at night.

"Well, that does it. Thanks, man. You want a beer or something?" Owen asks, setting the toolbox aside.

"I'm good. Thanks, though."

"What about dinner? You want to stay over? I'm sure we'll just order in, but you're more than welcome to stay."

I know what he's trying to do. Take pity on the

old single guy.

I shake my head. "Nah. Not tonight. Thanks, though."

Owen hesitates as if he has something else he wants to say. "Hey, so I know Ana's been living with you for a while now, and . . ."

I give him a blank look. "And?"

He swallows. "And I just want to make sure you're not in over your head with her. That you're not being taken advantage of."

I give him a stern look. "I'm not."

"I hate to say this, but are you really going to keep letting her live there rent-free once she has a kid? What about your own life?"

I take a deep breath, trying to slow my racing heart. My teammates have no idea the way I feel about Ana. They have no idea the things that have transpired between us over the past several months.

"I'm only going to say this once, because I trust you. Can you keep this to yourself?"

He nods, looking uncertain. "Of course, dude."

"Right now, Ana and I are just friends. But earlier on when she moved in . . . some things happened between us. And the baby . . . um, might be mine."

His eyes widen. "Oh. Damn. Wait… *Might?*"

I nod somberly. Part of me wishes I knew the truth too, but the other part of me doesn't care. Ana's important to me and so is her baby, regardless of whether it shares my DNA.

Owen breathes out. "Shit. I had no idea."

I nod. "I figured as much."

"So that's why she's still living there?"

I don't have an easier answer to his question. Swallowing my pride, I say, "She's welcome to stay as long as she wants, but she's mentioned getting her own place."

He nods, seeming to read something in my tone that hints at my unhappiness about the situation. "Anyone else know?"

"Pretty sure Jordie suspects it, but he hasn't pressed me for details."

"Well, I'm sorry if I came across as a dick. That wasn't my intention. I was just trying to look out for you."

"I know that," I say with a shrug.

Owen gives me another concerned look. "I know we haven't always been close, but I'm here, man. If you need anything. If you want to talk."

I nod. "Thanks. I'll keep that in mind."

"Anytime. And if you need any help or advice on baby stuff, you can ask, but be warned—I have no idea what I'm doing."

I chuckle, some of the tension of our conversation draining away. I know he really does mean well. "Thanks for that. I'll keep it in mind. And, hey, before I go, can I, uh, talk to Becca for a second?"

Owen scratches at the stubble on his neck. He's overdue for a shave. Then again, so are most hockey players. "Of course." He leads the way into the nursery where Becca is rocking their brand-new son in a gliding chair.

"Angel?" Owen's voice is softer than I've heard it before. It's a far cry from the Owen I know in the locker room. "Grant's here."

Her gaze lifts from her son's angelic face to mine. "Oh. Hey, Grant." She smiles weakly. She looks tired.

"He wanted to talk to you," Owen adds.

"Never mind if this is a bad time. I'll come back."

"It's not," she says around a yawn. "What's up?"

Owen gestures me over to the oversized navy ottoman across the room and I take a seat as he leaves us alone. It's only when I'm eye level with Becca do I notice that she's not just holding Bishop, she's nursing him.

My eyes dart away in a big damn hurry. "Jesus. I'm sorry. Seriously, I'll come back another time."

This makes her smile widen. "Calm down. It's a boob. I don't care if you don't."

I can feel my face turning warm, even though I thankfully can't see said boob. It's covered by a blanket and her son's head, but I can hear him suckling noisily on it like it's his last meal. It's kinda cute in a weird way.

I get it, buddy. I really do.

Boobs never stop being awesome. Doesn't matter if you're two weeks old or thirty-two. I still want them in my mouth too. *But not your mom's. Don't worry, little man.*

When I picture Ana nursing our baby, Ana murmuring soft sounds and cradling a swaddled lump in her arms, I get an achy feeling in the center of my chest.

"Just tell me what's on your mind," Becca says warmly.

Scrubbing one hand over the back of my neck, I consider this. "God, where to start." A dry, humorless chuckle pushes past my lips.

"This isn't about seeing me and Bishop, is it?" She grins.

"Um . . ." I hesitate, suddenly feeling unsure. Owen and Becca have just had their baby—a tiny, helpless little thing. They're probably exhausted and overwhelmed. And the visitors who have shown up have probably come bearing gifts and offering well wishes, not selfishly seeking advice like I am.

Before I can answer, she says, "It's okay if this is about Ana."

I smirk. "Am I that obvious?"

"Only to me."

I recall a conversation I overheard in the dressing room a few weeks ago.

"You don't think there's anything going on be-tween Grant and Ana, do you?"

"God, no. He would literally break her."

It was a funny observation—a six-foot-four dude with a petite girl like Ana. I can see how that would make people do a double-take. But no, I hadn't broken her. If anything, she'd broken me, but it's not like I could say that without inviting some serious questions. Questions I don't have the answers to. But I'm hoping to get some of those questions answered today.

With a deep inhale, I try to organize my thoughts. I've felt so scattered lately, so raw and helpless. I'm in way the fuck over my head with Ana and this pregnancy, and I don't like feeling so out of control.

"I just thought since you'd been through this recently, maybe you could tell me some things that might help. Like when she goes into labor . . ."

Becca nods. "Well, labor can be slow, or it can be fast. Everyone's different. But just be prepared, it can take a day, or even two. If she's comfortable with it, you could help out with back rubs or massaging her feet. Or even just being her advocate with the nurses."

I'm not even sure that Ana will want me in the hospital room, but I lean forward, placing my elbows on my knees. "Like how?"

"Well, like for instance, Owen was constantly asking the nurses questions, like when I needed more pain meds, or if I could have something to eat. It was nice not having to be the one to think about those things."

"Makes sense. What about delivery? She'll be in a lot of pain, right?"

Becca shifts, her mouth softening as she gazes down at Bishop for a second. "That depends. Do you know if she's planning to get an epidural?"

"I'm not sure."

Becca nods thoughtfully. "Natural childbirth is incredibly painful, but rewarding, from what I hear. I can only speak from my experience."

"Of course. So, what was it like?"

She touches Bishop's cheek with her index finger, lightly stroking it. "It wasn't as bad as I was expecting."

I nod. "Okay. That's promising."

She glances over at me. "This is going to sound

stupid . . ."

"Becca, it's not. I'm here pumping you for information about a woman I'm not even sure I'm dating."

"Stop." She frowns at me. "I know you're important to Ana."

"I don't know if I'd go that far."

"Well, I would." She gives me a pointed look. "But when she loses her mucus plug . . ."

My eyes widen. "Her what? Like a *plug* that pops out?"

She chuckles at my response. "It's not like a champagne cork, Grant. You know what? Never mind. It's just . . . once I lost mine, my labor came on quickly, but my experience was just that—*my* experience. So, why don't you just ask me what you came here to ask me?"

"I don't even know, to be honest. I just feel so useless all the time. What can I do? How can I be helpful to her?"

Becca lets out a little sigh and lifts Bishop, moving him to her other breast—and, *whoa*, this time I do get an eyeful, a flash of engorged boob and a swollen pink areola before quickly slamming my eyes shut.

Shit. This is weird.

"Grab me that burp cloth, would you?"

"Uh, sure." Rising to my feet, I grab the white cotton cloth printed with little green cacti and hand it to my teammate's wife while trying to wipe the image of her tit from my memory.

Once the baby is settled on the other side and sucking away happily again, Becca meets my eyes. "Well, if she wants space, you have to give her space. But you can let her know that you're there if she needs help."

She's right. I guess that's all I can do. I've re-spected Ana's desire to prove her independence, but it wouldn't hurt to make sure she knows my stance on things. I want to be by her side, even if it means laying my feelings bare. Even if it means possibly getting rejected again.

"You two all right in here?" Owen sticks his head through the open doorway and peeks inside.

"All good," I say.

"Bishop's done. Will you burp him?" Becca asks.

"Of course." Owen crosses the room in a few easy strides and lifts the baby from his wife's embrace.

She secures her top while I look down at my feet. When I look back up, Owen's got his miniature son perched high on his shoulder and is patting his back with gentle strokes. It's a sight I never thought I'd see—one of my teammates with a baby, those big, calloused hands being so tender. For a few seconds, I'm stunned speechless.

With a soft grunt, the baby lets out a wet-sounding burp. And then a fart.

We all laugh.

"He's definitely your son," Becca says lovingly, meeting Owen's eyes.

Owen only chuckles and coos some nonsense sounds to his son.

A hard knot pushes its way up my throat. I wasn't sure what to expect coming here today. They don't look frazzled or sleep-deprived like I might have thought. They look happy. Really happy.

Everything in this room is exactly what I want. A wife. A baby. A home filled with love and respect, and a shared sense of purpose. I've been alone my whole adult life. I'm ready for more, ready to settle down with a good woman.

But Becca's right—I can't force Ana. She has to *want* to choose me. And not just because some piece of paper says I'm the father of her baby, but because I'm the man she wants by her side.

And if she doesn't?

I have no fucking clue what I'll do.

CHAPTER TWENTY-THREE

Time to Go

Ana

Tapping the sides of my phone with my thumbs, I try to keep myself occupied with the little screen until Grant comes home from practice. He's running late, which he kindly told me via text message nearly forty minutes ago, so I went ahead and ate dinner without him. His portion sits in the fridge, waiting for him to come home.

Just like me, sitting at the kitchen counter, picking at a woven placemat with one finger . . . waiting for Grant to come home.

For the first time in a while, I regret opting out of the social media craze. It would be a nice escape to scroll through someone else's life for once. Instead, I'm laser focused on two pieces of information that I will be dutifully relaying to my lovely host and potential baby daddy.

It's a girl. I practice saying it without bursting into tears, mouthing the words silently.

I found out at today's appointment when the nurse showed me the ultrasound photos. I didn't want to know at first and kind of put it off, but today I was ready for them to tell me. It seems all the more real the bigger my belly grows.

The sight of that little nugget paired with the knowledge that I'm the mom of a tiny, precious little girl completely destroyed any resolve I had going in. I wept for joy in front of the ill-equipped nurse, who left me with a box of tissues to cry it out for as long as I needed to. And cry I did. I wasn't even sure why I was so emotional—maybe because this all finally feels real.

Now, the second piece of information isn't nearly as miraculous. Earlier this month, I found a small two-bedroom apartment in Wedgewood, just a few miles north of Grant's condo. It's cozy and semi-furnished, with a brick interior, tons of natural light, and a dog-friendly courtyard. Perfect for me. I contacted the landlord and worked out the particulars, dropping a sizable amount of this month's paycheck on the initial security deposit. Which wouldn't have been possible without all the extra income I've saved living with Grant rent-free.

Today, I got the confirmation that I can move in as early as tomorrow. With most of my belongings already packed away into boxes, it only took me an hour to get my travel bag packed and ready. I'm all set to go. Now I just need to tell Grant.

I'm zoning out, completely lost in the blurry photo I asked the nurse to snap of the ultrasound machine's screen, when the front door opens. Hobbes barrels from the back of the condo, where he was up to God knows what, and makes himself a nuisance at Grant's feet.

I lean from my spot at the counter, calling out, "Hey!"

"Hey," comes Grant's response between murmurs to the dog. When he finally comes into my line of sight, he has a panting, elated Hobbes tucked under one arm.

My heart warms at the odd pair and their bizarre friendship. *Who knew?*

"Sorry I'm late." Grant sighs, his hair wind-blown and his cheekbones red with Seattle chill.

My impulse is to jump up and smooth his hair for him, brush those cheeks with my fingertips . . .

but instead, I sit on my hands.

"You're fine." I smile, nodding my head to the fridge. "Your dinner is in there. It's quiche." *A variation on the very meal he made for me the first night I stayed here.*

"Awesome." Grant chuckles, setting Hobbes down on the floor, who whines in dismay.

There's a comfortable silence for a few minutes as I watch Grant putter around the kitchen, poking his head in the fridge, carrying his plate to the microwave, and filling a tall glass with water as the microwave thrums with the promise of a hot dinner.

With my elbow propped on the counter, I lean my cheek against my knuckles. I love watching this man, this *superhero* of a human, operate like a regular person. The way his giant hand wraps around the tiny microwave handle, all while juggling his drink and a small bowl of salad in the other, makes me giggle. His eyes are twinkling with good humor when he joins me, making himself comfortable next to me at the counter with a relieved sigh.

"What are you smiling about?"

"Oh, if you must know . . . you," I say weakly, trying to contain the sadness quickly overtaking my voice.

Of course Grant sees right through me. He finishes chewing his first bite, his eyes narrowed in an *I know you better than that* way.

"What's the matter?" he asks, setting his fork down.

"Do you recognize those flavors?" I say, pointing to his steaming plate. Ignoring well-intentioned questions isn't my usual move, but I'm desperate for a little small talk. *Just to start.*

Grant opens his mouth to call me out on my subject change, but thinks better of it. With one eyebrow adorably quirked up and the other down, he inspects the quiche with the concentration of a detective on his most gruesome case yet. I cover my smile with my fingers.

"Sure," he finally says. "Eggs, tomatoes, green peppers, cheese, and . . . onions."

"The first night I stayed here, you made me an omelet with those very same ingredients," I murmur softly, tapping the counter space between us.

Grant reaches across the quartz surface, catching my fingers in his big strong hand. "That's right," he says, caressing my knuckles with a soft squeeze that I feel in my heart.

He doesn't realize how hard he's making this.

"What's the occasion?" he asks, dipping his head a little to catch my downcast eyes.

"Well . . . I'm moving out," I say softly.

Grant's thumb halts its dance across my knuckles. He releases me, his back straightening. "I'm aware. Have you still been looking for a place? We could tour a few places in the neighborhood."

"I'm actually moving tomorrow morning to a small place in Wedgewood."

"Tomorrow?" Grant rarely looks surprised, so the shock on his face hits me hard in the gut.

I knew I should have told him sooner.

"Yes, I've been thinking about this for a while. I just wanted to tell you in person."

"I see."

He leans back, somehow closer to the guarded man who first took me in, and further from the kind, intuitive soul I know him to be.

How can I fix this?

"Hey, look on the bright side," I say with a fake smile. "You'll get your bachelor pad back."

"You mean I'll be alone again."

His eyes are searing with emotion, catching me completely off guard. I feel my own eyes pricking with tears, and a lump forming in my throat.

"I need to do this, Grant. I need to take care of myself and stand on my own two feet. Don't get me wrong; I'm forever indebted to you for carrying me this far. But if I'm planning to bring another life into this world . . . well, I need to know that I can take care of myself first."

All that talking, and the lump in my throat still hasn't subsided. Grant listens to my speech with a solemn expression on his face. Finally, he gives me one solitary nod, a small smile cracking through his stoic defenses.

"Will you at least let me help you move?"

I grimace. Every time I open my mouth, I say something that completely crushes him. *I hate this.*

"Actually, Owen, Jordie, and Justin are coming by before practice."

Grant leans back, releasing a pained sigh. I didn't think about how much it might hurt him that

I asked his teammates for help rather than ask him. Maybe I can salvage this.

"I was going to ask you'd help us load the boxes into Jordie's truck," I say, a sheepish grin forming on my lips.

Grant, meanwhile, seems unconvinced.

I reach across the counter again, touching his hand. "I would really love your help, Grant."

When he meets my eyes, the emotion I see in them is almost too much to handle. "Of course I'll help you."

"Thank you." I squeeze his hand. "There's something else I want to tell you."

"What is it?" he asks, obviously bracing himself for another bombshell.

I smile. "It's a girl."

Grant's defenses crumble, his eyes widening. "A girl?"

"Yeah."

He doesn't say anything else, but his eyes tell me the whole story. I hold his gaze, a single tear escaping my eye. As badly as I want to look away and hide from the enormous *feeling* lingering behind his eyes, I don't. The moment simmers with emotion, and I can't deny there's a little voice inside asking if I'm sure.

I swallow and break eye contact.

I have to do this, have to be certain I'm capable of taking care of myself.

• • •

With all but a handful of boxes unpacked, my new apartment is looking more and more put together by the second.

The team did an astounding job of moving my belongings from Grant's, to the truck, across town, and up two flights of stairs. Sure, we got a few odd looks from Owen and Justin when they walked into Grant's condo to see all my things piled neatly by the front door. After I explained that their team captain had been kind enough to hold on to most of my things when I was displaced by the breakup, Grant just had to bark a few orders to get their bug eyes focused on the project at hand.

Hobbes sat, quivering anxiously in my lap for the whole ordeal.

Overall, the guys were done in two hours and off to morning practice. I spent the day unpacking and arranging . . . and rearranging. It's been so long since I've been able to make the decisions in my own home.

It's nice.

My phone buzzes. It's Becca, letting me know that she's not going to be able to make it to my housewarming tonight. *Understandably, what with a newborn baby.*

The plans came together rather suddenly when a few of the hockey wives wanted to show their support in their own way. Several long hours of unloading my life and one group chat later, I'm expecting Elise, Sara, and Bailey at seven o'clock.

Normally, I'd be overwhelmed by the attention. But I'm honestly excited for a little female companionship. Georgia has been busy with work, and she's the first to admit that she's a little freaked out by the whole baby thing, so I'm giving her space.

Tonight will be refreshing, if nothing else. Besides, Elise has made serious promises of pizza delivery, and I'm starving.

The kitchen is mostly unpacked and organized, being my favorite room in any living situation. I'm too daunted by my lack of baby necessities to touch the nursery yet. The living room (or maybe it's a den?) is suitable enough for company. I just hope no one wants a tour, because my bedroom isn't ready for guests.

After breaking down a couple more empty cardboard boxes, I carry them to the alley, a leashed Hobbes leading the way. After a long walk around the block—long enough to let him sniff every exciting new twig, leaf, and fire hydrant—we head back home. I fumble awkwardly with my new keys. *You'll get used to them.*

When I get the door open, Hobbes tears inside, a completely new dog compared to the timid little thing he was this morning. He rounds the whole apartment, coming to a halt at my feet with a wagging tongue to match his tail.

I scoop him into my arms, eliciting a happy yip. Together, we plop down onto the couch for an impromptu cuddle session. I don't realize how exhausted I am until I sink into the plush cushions of the couch. I'm a goner before I know it.

• • •

I wake up to the sound of an apartment buzzer. I jolt upright, unfamiliar with the tone. Hobbes runs to the window, barking. With a little effort, I push myself up from the couch, hobbling to the intercom.

"Hello?"

The voices that come through are scrambled and very, *very* enthusiastic.

"Ana—babe— Can—let—in? Downstairs—"

"Come in, come in!" I laugh as I punch the door button, and soon I hear the sounds of three pairs of feet charging up the stairs.

Elise is the first to enter when I open the door.

"Oh my God, Ana! This place is perfect," she says with a gasp. She reaches out to squeeze my arm while her gaze travels from one wall to another.

"It's a good size," Sara says with a smile and a nod, stepping in just behind Elise. "Hi, Ana. Thanks for having us."

I get a whiff of an enviable perfume when she leans in to hug me.

"Of course," I say with a smile, closing the door after Bailey steps in, all smiles and wide eyes. My place is kind of cramped with this much energy. But it's nice too. It was really quiet before.

"Hi, puppy!" Bailey kneels down immediately

to pamper Hobbes, who attacks her fingers with kisses of the sloppy variety. She looks up at me with a question on her lips.

"How are you feeling?" Bailey, the doctor, asks. She looks me up and down, and I find myself smoothing my tousled hair.

"Sleepy, mostly," I say with a chuckle.

"That's totally normal." Bailey gives me her dazzling smile.

"That's a relief." I sigh and wave the women toward the couch. "I haven't had time to set up the TV, but I've got my laptop if you want some background noise."

"Speaking of background noise," Elise says in a singsong voice, pulling a small package from her purse wrapped in bright yellow tissue paper with white polka dots.

A gift? "What's that?"

"Open it!" Elise practically squeals, tossing the package to me and plopping down on the couch. There are a couple other presents—a dark pink envelope resting on Sara's knees and a purple gift bag resting at Bailey's feet.

What's going on?

With a little suspicion in my expression, I carefully unwrap the present, revealing a high-tech baby monitor that promises to hook up with my phone. It looks expensive.

"Oh my gosh," I whisper, searching for answers in the expectant faces of my friends. I clasp the gift to my heart and struggle to find words.

"You look like you're about to have a heart attack. It's just a little informal baby shower for an amazing woman," Sara says matter-of-factly, giving me a warm look.

"We wanted to spoil you!" Bailey cries out, beaming from the couch cushions. "Please let us."

That pesky lump is making a home in my throat again, and my eyes are welling up with tears. These dang hormones have me crying 24/7.

"You guys didn't have to do that."

After several protests that, *yes*, they did indeed have to do that, I open the other two presents. From Sara, I receive a gift card to a local baby boutique for a dollar amount that makes my jaw drop. *Oh, to have an attorney's salary . . .*

"Their stuff is pretty damn cute, or you could just blow it all on a top-of-the-line stroller," Sara says with a sly smile.

I reach out to her with both arms, wrapping her in a tight hug. "Thank you," I whisper.

She rubs my back comfortingly. "You got it, babe," she whispers back with a chuckle.

"Me next!" Bailey chirps, shoving a gift bag at me with an enthusiasm I'll never replicate.

Tossing the tissue paper to the side, I discover an assortment of small, thoughtful gifts: a baby thermometer, seven cloth diapers, a package that contains bottles with an assortment of different-sized nipples, a plush elephant stuffed animal, and a soft gray blanket.

Rubbing the material of the exquisitely soft blanket between thumb and forefinger, I look up at Bailey, who watches me with a knowing grin.

"I'm gonna love your kid so much." Bailey sighs happily. "I can already tell."

"Aww," I coo, melting. "Come here! All of you, come here."

They do, wrapping me in their arms and soothing scent. Cloaked in the warmth of my friends' embrace, I smile as Hobbes curls up against my feet. I've never felt safer or more at peace. *Well . . .*

except for when I'm curled up in bed with a certain mountain of muscle.

"I have to ask," Sara says once we've untangled our mess of limbs. "What's going on with you and Grant?"

Elise chimes in before I can even open my mouth. "Yeah! Justin said he'd been housing all of your stuff in his fancy condo ever since you-know-who got demoted."

"Good fucking riddance," Bailey says.

I flash them all an appreciative smile. *Agreed.*

"Grant has been . . . a really, really good friend to me."

"Just a friend?" Sara's eyes narrow on me in that scary lawyer way.

Before I can come up with another non-answer, the door buzzes.

"That must be the pizza!" Elise says.

When no one makes a move to answer the door, I remember that this my apartment and that would be my job.

"Oh! I—I'll get it," I stammer, my cheeks warm. The other girls chuckle amongst themselves, but not in a mean way. I don't mind the teasing, actually.

I'm digging through my wallet for small bills to tip the guy when I swing open the door.

"Hey, hold on one second—"

"Pizza's here!" Becca bellows as she parades through the door, holding the pizza box high over her head.

I drop my wallet in shock, covering a gasp with my hands. "Becca?"

The women in the living room positively roar with laughter. Becca charges ahead and sets the pizza down on the coffee table before them, turning to take a bow.

"I thought you weren't coming!"

"It was a surprise. I didn't have time to buy you anything, so this is my present to you," Becca says, gesturing to herself. Stepping toward me and placing two warm, pizza-scented hands on my shoulders, she gives me a very stern look. "Ana."

I stand at attention, my eyes locked on Becca's.

"I am an exhausted mother of a crazy newborn gremlin," she says. "I'm tired and emotional all the time. I'm a walking corpse. But I'm also living proof that your life will not end when you have a baby. You will still go out, you will still have fun, and you will still have your friends at your side through it all."

I choke on a sob, covering my face with my hands. *What did I do to deserve these friends?*

"You made her cry!" Elise says, mockingly accusing Becca.

"She'll be fine." Becca laughs, pulling me into her arms and rocking me from side to side.

Yes. She'll be just fine.

CHAPTER TWENTY-FOUR
Cherished

Ana

When I look down, I can't see my toes anymore. My belly is so big, so full of life. It's so big, in fact, that I had to call Grant to help me set up the crib. This baby is due in less than eight weeks now, and judging by the way she's doing entire dance routines in there, she's eager to make her entrance into the world.

I can only hope to match her level of energy when she's no longer confined to my womb. Watching Grant put the crib together on the floor of the otherwise bare nursery, I remind myself that I won't be alone.

"Can I help in any way?" I ask, nervously rubbing my belly. That's a new thing, the belly rubbing. It's almost compulsive at this stage.

"Absolutely not." Grant grunts, poking his head out from under the wooden contraption with a sly grin.

My heart flip-flops. Pregnancy hormones have magnified all the attraction I have toward this man, and let me tell you, it is *distracting*.

"Okay," I say, conceding for only a moment. "How about tea? Would you like some tea?"

Grant eyes me from his vantage point on the floor. Seeing how desperate I am to help, he nods. "I could drink some tea."

"Caffeinated?"

"Whatever."

"Coming right up." I toddle off to the kitchen, happy to have a mission.

My phone sits untouched on the kitchen counter, abandoned, tossed aside after a tense call with Jason earlier today. I'd reached out, stupidly, to ask for his new Wisconsin address.

Earlier this week, the two paternity test kits I ordered arrived at my doorstep. I bought them on a whim . . . an emotionally unstable whim, perhaps. A big part of me doesn't want to know who the biological father of this sweet, innocent child is. A big, cowardly part. And I can't decide whether it's because I want Grant to be the father, or because I *don't* want Jason to be.

Months ago, when I told Jason over the phone that I was pregnant, his reaction was to be expected. Are you sure? How is that possible? Did you mess up your birth control? What am I supposed to do? I just moved here, do you expect me to move back?

After assuring him that I had it all under control and only reached out to him as a courtesy, I hung up, cried for an hour, and got the hell on with my life. But that's not to say it's been easy.

Everything sets me off these days, even well-meaning strangers when they make comments about how excited my husband and I must be.

"Don't have one of those," I always say.

"Oh, your boyfriend then," they say with a tight-lipped smile.

"Don't have one of those either."

Just as before, the phone conversation Jason and I had earlier this morning was quick and strained. I should have known better. Asking him to take a paternity test could only lead to one thing—him accusing me of cheating on him.

"Why would you need that? Were you fucking someone else?" he spat out, his voice as harsh as I remember it getting during our worst fights.

And to think he might have changed.

"For the record, that's none of your business, Jason," I said with a clipped tone. "But no, I did not cheat on you, and I would really appreciate it if you could take this. For me."

"I'll bet you would."

"Jason, please."

"Not until you tell me the truth."

I ended the call, then and there. Jason doesn't deserve to know about Grant. He doesn't deserve to know *anything* about my life anymore. *Bastard.*

Listening to the low whistle of the teakettle warming on the stove, I check my phone for the first time in hours. Two missed calls from Jason, naturally, and a text from Georgia.

Thinking about you. Let me know if you have energy for a girls' night. I'll come to you! Can't wait to see the new place. xoxo

The message warms my heart. *God, I've missed her.* We still see each other at work, of course, but we haven't hung out in months.

I've been giving her space since I dropped the baby bomb on her, uncertain of how she'd react. Looks like our friendship is going to be just fine, after all.

The kettle whistles loudly, pulling me back into the present. Armed with a warm mug of mint tea, I reenter the nursery. The crib is upright and secured, from what I can tell. But Grant's nowhere to be seen. *Odd.*

I hear the front door open and peek my head out into the hall. Grant shuffles inside, two giant woven baskets in his arms, filled to the brim with shopping bags. He looks up and catches my eye, knowing he's been caught.

He smiles, a big goofy grin. "Had to make a trip to the car. Got you a few things this morning."

I roll my eyes playfully, unable to stop the smile spreading across my lips. *I swear to God, this man has no boundaries.* I'd be lying if I said I didn't love it.

For the next hour, we set up the nursery, embellishing the walls with decorative baby animal portraits, filling the dresser drawers with fresh cotton sheets and fleece blankets for the crib, and putting night-lights and protective covers in every available outlet. By the end, I'm sweating a bit, hands on my hips as I admire the nursery, which now looks like it was ripped straight from the pages of a magazine.

Grant takes a sip of his now lukewarm tea and nods in approval. "There's one more thing," he says, already on his way down the hall toward the front door.

"Can I help?" I call, rubbing my belly anxiously. *I hope it's nothing too big.*

"I got it!"

What he carries through the door, not five minutes later, brings the whole damn world to a halt.

"How?" I let out a shocked breath, leaning against the wall for support as I watch with wide, teary eyes as Grant carries my mother's chestnut rocking chair down the hall. *Oh my God.*

"I reached out to your dad," Grant says as he walks the chair into the nursery, positioning it in the corner between the hamper baskets. "I hope you don't mind. I just know how close you were with your mom, and wanted to see if that rocking chair you were telling me about was still around. He was happy to help. I had it shipped here and picked it up yesterday."

While he explains, I walk up to the old, familiar chair, touching one curved arm with shaking fingertips. Grant steps away to give me space, but that's the last thing I want right now. *What I want is him.*

"Come here," I say, my arms outstretched and my eyes misty with emotion.

Grant complies, stepping into my arms and wrapping his own around me, careful not to squeeze too tightly. My heart hammers, my breaths shaky and uneven.

"Thank you." I sniffle wetly into his shirt.

He runs his hand over my hair, still holding me close. "You're welcome," he murmurs, his lips pressed to the top of my head.

I pull back, searching his eyes. He towers over me, a pillar of strength I've come to depend on. And for once, I'm starting to think that's okay.

Standing up on my tippy-toes, I pull Grant down to me with a gentle tug of his shirt. When our lips meet, all the time apart vanishes in an instant, and I'm sucked right back in time.

I wrap my arms around his neck, straining for him, straining for his kiss. Grant cups my cheek, his mouth covering mine in a hungry kiss. Outside the nursery window, rain begins to patter against the glass, another storm rolling in. He pulls back, resting his forehead against mine as our panting breaths collide between us.

"It's raining," he says softly.

"I know."

"Are you okay?" he asks, his eyes dark with passion, but his brow is creased with familiar concern.

"I'm perfect." I sigh happily, brushing my lips to his again. "Are you?"

"Yes," he says with a growl, and presses his lips to mine.

I'm dizzy, drunk from his taste and smell and the feel of him in my arms. And despite my balloon of a belly, I can feel his kiss all the way down to my toes.

"Do you want to go to my bedroom?" I choke out, gasping when Grant finds a particularly sensitive spot on my jaw in his slow journey toward my neck.

"Yes." He groans, clearly wishing we were there already.

Normally, I'd be happy to get down and dirty on the floor. But with this belly, I need some support.

"Let's go." I giggle, pulling him by one hand out of the nursery. I turn back to him with a smirk when we reach my door. "Don't judge, okay? My body doesn't look like it used to."

"You're beautiful, Ana," Grant whispers into my ear, sending chill bumps racing down my spine.

Once inside my room, he spins me around, but not too fast. I'm a little top-heavy, so he's sure to handle me with care. Untying my maternity dress with slow, steady fingers, he continues whispering sweet nothings into my ear.

"You're fucking gorgeous, you know that? You knock me out."

Eager to show him exactly how beautiful I think *he* is, I press my hands under the hem of his shirt, needing to feel the warmth of his skin, to touch those deliciously defined muscles again. Grant releases me only for as long as it takes to rip his shirt off, his hair tousled and his eyes wild with desire. I press my face to his pecs, flicking my tongue out to taste him. His chest vibrates with a deep, guttural moan as he slides his fingers into my hair.

"Let's lie down," he says, his voice hoarse.

I can tell he'd like nothing more than to bend me over my dresser and take me right here and now, and truth be told, that very fantasy has played in my head more than once. However, I'm startlingly pregnant, so however we're going to do this will have to be one hundred percent safe for both me and the baby.

Grant strips out of his pants before sitting down on the edge of my bed, where he watches me peel the maternity dress from my shoulders and drop it to my ankles. In my underwear, I've never felt quite so exposed in my life. And o*h God . . .* they're *maternity* underwear.

Just kill me now.

"Come here," he murmurs, one of his hands gently massaging his bulging erection through the cotton of his briefs. It's distracting as all hell.

My heart skitters as I watch him. He's so bulky and gorgeous and just . . . big all over. I step closer until I'm standing in between his powerful thighs.

When my gaze lands on his, his eyes are filled with adoration and desire, and there's nothing but heat between us. Without breaking our eye contact, he reaches behind me to unclasp my bra. It falls to the floor, joining my dress. My heartbeat is so fast and loud, I'm not sure how he doesn't hear it, but Grant stays focused. He's looking at me like I'm the best, most desirable thing he's ever seen.

His eyes are dark with pleasure, and the way he watches me sends chills racing down my body. It's hard to breathe with him looking at me like that. And then his gaze drops lower, settling at my breasts, and he sucks in a ragged breath. They're larger than they've ever been. And more sensitive too.

"Oh fuck, these things are amazing." His voice is raspy, full of hot emotion.

Cupping the weight of one lush breast, Grant rubs his thumb across my nipple. A bolt of heat sizzles down my spine. He leans forward and kisses the top of one breast, then the other, and I release a shaky exhale.

When he sucks one perky nipple into his mouth, I tremble. And when he sucks the other just as firmly into his hot mouth, I almost fall apart on the spot. It's too much sensation, and not enough at the same time. The rough scratch of his stubble creates a welcome sting, and I moan, arching my back to get even closer.

Reaching out, I stroke his eager erection through the fabric. "Grant . . ." I moan as he nuzzles into my breasts. "I need you," I say with a stuttered breath.

His eyes meet mine with a solemn expression that for a second I can't read. Everything grows quiet between us, and the moment drags on with uncertainty.

Does he not want to? Maybe I'm too pregnant.

Oh God . . . My face heats in embarrassment.

His fingertips skim over my hips as he admires me, and his Adam's apple bobs as he swallows. "I don't have a condom."

Oh. "I don't care." I pause and then look at him again. "Unless I should?"

He shakes his head. "I haven't been with anyone else."

"Me either." The second the words leave my mouth, his lips quirk up, and I realize how ridiculous that sounds. I'm nearly eight months pregnant. It kind of goes without saying that suitors aren't exactly lining up around the block for me.

"Come here," he says on another groan.

I sit down on the edge of the bed, holding my belly with one hand and using the other to help lower my torso onto the bed, until I'm nestled into his arms. My back is to him, but that doesn't deter him one bit. Before I can try to turn, his hot breath is in my ear again.

"Are you comfortable?" he asks, his hands seeking my most sensitive spots, cupping my breasts again, caressing my cleavage, my nipples . . . my belly.

"Yes." I moan, loving the way his huge, warm hands envelop my belly, making me feel so small again. So protected.

Grant kisses my neck and shoulder, his tongue drawing lazy circles across my tender flesh in the most distracting way. I press my ass into his engorged cock, which twitches excitedly against the soft material of my underwear. His hand slips into the front of my panties, and he lets out a low growl.

"How do you want me?" he asks, pulling his hands away to slide his briefs down his legs.

"Like this." I whimper, bumping my backside

against the firm ridge in his boxer briefs again.

With deft fingers, Grant pulls my underwear down my legs. Bringing his hand between my thighs, he presses gently against my clit. I gasp, bucking into his hand, absolutely wild for that delicious friction.

I reach back, one hand touching the hair at the nape of his neck, and the other grabbing his ass. He obeys my unspoken command, lining himself up with my warm, wet center.

"Tell me if I'm going too fast," he murmurs, his lips at the back of my neck.

"You're not. Please," I say on a needy groan.

He moves with slow, purposeful intention, pressing forward inch by broad inch until I'm so full of him, I can hardly breathe.

I cry out, rocking my hips into his, deepening our connection. He feels incredible, and hot lust rolls through me, pushing away every thought and worry I've had over the last few weeks.

I wanted to learn to stand on my own two feet, and I have, but that doesn't mean I don't have needs. And right now, my pregnancy hormones are dictating that I need this right here. His strong arms around me, his rigid body moving inside of mine.

Grant nibbles on my neck, pumping in and out while he rubs my clit with expert precision. Only a few minutes later, I feel my orgasm barreling toward me. *Holy unexpected . . .*

"I'm c-coming." I gasp, the waves crashing over me harder and faster than I've ever experienced.

Grant grabs one of my plump breasts as he fucks me into his own orgasm, a strangled moan filling my ear as he empties himself inside me. We're a sweaty, breathless mess for the next few minutes, both of us just trying to slow our heart rate while we listen to the rain fall outside.

"Wow," I choke out, still panting.

"Yeah," he says, gathering me close.

"Could you help me turn over?"

Grant complies, helping me sit up and shift my body so that I'm now facing him. We curl into each other like we've done this our entire lives.

"How do you feel?" he asks, one hand reaching down to caress my belly.

"I feel amazing," I say with a chuckle.

"Me too." He smiles, pressing his lips to my forehead in a precious kiss.

"I wasn't sure if sex while pregnant would work," I say. "It seemed unlikely with another . . . *being* in the room."

"True." Grant laughs, smoothing my hair from my cheek and neck. "Third parties aside . . . I think you wear it well."

"The belly?" I ask, incredulous.

"You're sexy as hell." He sighs, touching his lips to mine. "It's been tough."

"Has it?" I laugh, my eyebrows raised.

"You have no idea."

"I'm sure I have some idea," I whisper against his lips.

We kiss then, long and slow and perfectly in sync. It's the kind of kiss that I doubt I'll ever forget.

"I have a gift for you too," I say once we part.

"You do?" His voice is surprised.

"I'd get it for you, but I don't think I'll be moving from this spot for a minute."

"Where is it?"

"On the dresser."

Grant plants a firm kiss against my forehead before he vaults out of bed, younger now than I've ever seen him act. I watch him (well, his muscular butt) as he saunters over to the dresser, finding the box and lifting it.

"This?"

"That's the one."

He looks at it for a minute, reading the sans serif type on the front, and then on the back, and then on the front again.

After what feels like a year has passed, I speak up. "What do you think?"

"It's a DNA test?"

"Yes."

"Why?" he asks, sounding confused but not irritated.

"Well, don't you want to know if she's yours?" I ask, tapping my fingers across my swollen belly.

He stares for a prolonged moment before setting the box down on the dresser and climbing back into bed with me. "I hate to say this after you've already spent money . . . but I don't need that thing," he says softly, his fingertips resting lightly on my arm, drawing inscrutable patterns.

"Why not?"

"I just . . ." He sighs, thinking for a moment before he shrugs. "I don't care. She's *yours*. And that's good enough for me."

"You don't . . . *care*?" I brace myself for the impossible hurt I know is about to hit me.

"I don't. I'm going to love and care for this child, regardless of whether she's mine or someone else's. It doesn't matter to me. She's your baby, Ana, and I plan to protect and care for both you and your child for as long as you'll have me."

For the umpteenth time today, tears well up in my eyes, a fountain of gratitude pouring from me. *What am I supposed to say to that?*

"Okay," I whisper through the tears.

"Okay." Grant chuckles, reaching over to the bedside table to grab a tissue. He wipes my wet cheeks and my nose with a tenderness I almost can't believe for such a large man.

"In that case . . . can you do one more thing for

me?" I ask, batting my eyelashes.

"Anything."

"Can you help me get up so I can go pee?"

His broad shoulders vibrate with a deep, echo-ing laugh. "You bet."

CHAPTER TWENTY-FIVE

Change of Heart

Grant

"**D**on't say a word," I grumble, lacing up my skates.

Jordie raises both hands in surrender. "Not saying a thing." He grins wickedly. "Other than . . . you look *so pretty*."

I flip him the middle finger. I got a black eye during our last game. Fucking Vancouver Rebels. Hooligans, the whole team. And since the director of the charity organization thought I would, and I quote, *scare the children,* I'm now wearing fucking makeup to cover it.

Apparently, between my unkempt beard and the black eye, I'm a scary motherfucker these days. And so when I arrived for the Little Rookies camp today, the director marched me straight back into the dressing room and grabbed something from her purse, all but shoving me into a metal folding chair. I didn't realize it was makeup until she was halfway through. I opened my mouth to protest, but she went right on dabbing and blending until the bruise under my eye had mostly vanished.

"Dude, get over here." Morgan, our backup goalie, cackles like a hyena. "Cap's wearing make-up."

I grimace at them. "Apparently, my appearance was going to frighten the kids."

Jordie chuckles. "Yeah, but now you're a six-foot-four dude with a grizzly-ass beard who also wears makeup, so what's worse?"

"Fuck off, Jordie."

He shrugs. "Fair enough."

We take our places on the ice, which quiets down my teammates, although I'm sure I haven't heard the last of this. I'm assigned to work with the younger group of kids, so I head over to the far end to get my station set up.

The ice has been configured in stations with foam pads sectioning it off into quadrants, and there are nets positioned in each corner to create more scoring opportunities. It makes me wish a program like this existed when I first started.

Watching a dozen five- and six-year-olds waddle and scoot their way out across the ice in full hockey gear puts a smile on my face. The feeling is so foreign, because I haven't smiled since Ana moved out two weeks ago.

"Hey, mister!" one of the little boys with two missing teeth calls, gazing up at me.

"Yeah?" I bend down so I can meet his eyes through the cage on his helmet.

"What happened to your face?"

I chuckle. "Nothing, kid, I'm fine. You want to practice shooting the puck or what?"

"Yeah!" he shouts and toddles off toward the net, barely avoiding tripping over his own stick along the way.

I skate behind him, trying not to get hit in the nuts with any stray sticks or pucks.

There's not much actual instruction with this age level, just some occasional praise and a lot of picking kids up off the ice when they fall. I spend the next forty-five minutes working with the group while my mind wanders to Ana and my unborn baby. Somewhere along the way, I started thinking of the baby as mine.

No matter what some DNA test or piece of paper might say, I know how I feel about Ana and the child growing inside her.

The parents who raised me didn't do so out of biological obligation, and that didn't make them any less my mom and dad. As a result, I never felt the need to go looking for my birth parents. I understood the reasoning of why some people feel compelled to, but I've never had that urge.

All I want is for Ana to give me a shot at a future, because I'm pretty damn certain we could be the real deal if she'd only try.

Holding her in my arms the other night, and the feel of her belly between us. Watching her fall apart when I brought over the rocking chair her mother used when she was a baby. And then, *God*, making love to her after—it was an incredible night.

But the idea of her still wanting space . . . the idea of her doing all this on her own . . . it makes me feel like punching something. I've tried to be patient, tried to give her space and still be there for her when she needs me. It's a lot. It's a damn good thing I have hockey to distract me.

The season is still in full swing, but before long, it'll be coming to an end. We've done well, but it doesn't look like we'll make the playoffs, which should disappoint me. But since Ana's due date is in June, I'm oddly relieved by this fact. I wouldn't want to try to juggle the Stanley Cup playoffs and a new baby at the same time.

Watching these little ones skate around, I find it easy to remember myself as a kid. I grew up without much, but I always had hockey. And now, now that I'm getting older . . . I want something steady in my life. I want Ana. And our baby.

Realizing that the charity director is trying to get my attention, I skate over toward where she's standing with a clipboard at the edge of the ice.

"If you could get everyone's attention and have them gather around," she says with a smile. "Your voice is louder than mine, I'm sure."

I nod. "Sure thing."

Skating toward center ice again, I call out to the guys that it's time to wrap up. Soon, dozens of miniature hockey players and the other coaches are skating toward the exit where she waits, still holding her clipboard.

"Good job out there today, everyone," she says.

"Hockey is a sport that requires mental toughness, determination, and focus. And the most important quality of all—someone who won't give up."

As I listen to her talk, I realize the same could be said about my relationship with Ana—determination and not giving up are things I'm good at. But then I remember Becca's advice . . . that if Ana wants space, I'll need to respect that. It might suck, but it's true. I can't force myself on her.

But even if she doesn't want a relationship with me, she can't legally keep my child from me. Pursuing legal custody isn't a road I want to venture down. I want her to choose me—to choose us. But if she won't? I may have no choice but to take that test and get the court involved.

Because after interacting with these kids today? There's no way in hell I'm going to miss out on the chance to be a dad.

CHAPTER TWENTY-SIX

Game Time

Ana

"**O**uch." I groan and rub at a tender spot in my lower back. I've been puttering around the kitchen for the past hour, cleaning compulsively to take my mind off of how weird I've felt all morning. Well, weird is probably the wrong word. I've felt crampy and had a backache for the last two hours.

I take a deep, shaky breath, and touch the firm bump of my belly.

Contractions. I guess that's what these are.

My heart hammering, I reach for my phone.

"Hello?" Grant's deep voice offers me some temporary peace.

"Hi," I say, intensely relieved. "I'm so glad you answered."

"We're on break. Are you all right?" He sounds a little out of breath. I knew he'd be at practice.

"I think I'm going into labor."

There's a brief pause on the other end of the line. Before I can check the connection, I can hear Grant speaking to someone nearby. It's muffled, but I can make out "have to leave now" and "tell Coach."

"I'm on my way," he says gruffly into the phone.

In the background, I hear the familiar rustle of his hockey bag. Strange how comforting that sound has become. It's a sound I used to associate with Jason, but now all I can think about when I hear it is the early morning sounds of Grant getting ready for practice before I manage to force myself out of bed.

"Thank you," I whisper, lowering myself to the floor. The cool tile helps me feel a little more control in this otherwise bananas situation.

I can't believe it's happening already. There's still a week to go until my due date.

"Are you okay? Do you want me to call an ambulance?"

"I'm okay," I say weakly, but with a smile. "I think as long as you get here within the next twenty minutes, I'll be fine."

"I'll make it in ten. Stay on the phone with me, okay?"

"Okay." I let out a grateful breath.

For as long as it takes Grant to drive from the training facility to my apartment, we stay on the phone. Alternating between breathing exercises and joking about my live-in caretaker, Hobbes, slacking on his job, Grant keeps me focused on the present. Meanwhile, Hobbes has curled up against my thigh, his tail wagging excitedly. He sniffs my belly and looks up at me curiously. Hobbes may be more ready for this baby than I am.

In record time, Grant walks through the door. He's on his knees before me, even before Hobbes can jump up to greet him.

"Hey there," he murmurs, tucking loose, wild strands of hair behind my ears.

"Hi." I smile. "We should go."

"Where's your hospital bag?"

"By the front door."

Grant helped me pack a bag for the hospital a few weeks ago when he stopped by for a visit. He also brought me a pie on that visit. He's been so good to me, even when all I've done is repeatedly push him away.

"It's going to be okay," he reminds me, sensing my nervousness. He helps me off the floor, leading me to the door and helping me slip my comfiest flats onto my swollen feet as Hobbes circles our legs anxiously.

"I'll be back for you," Grant tells him, leaning down to ruffle his soft fur.

Then Grant grabs my bag, which contains a robe and slippers, some toiletries, an extra phone charger . . . the works. Plus diapers and baby outfits I picked especially for the occasion. I've been ready for this moment for a while now, but somehow with each passing second, I feel less prepared than ever.

The stairs prove to be tricky, so Grant gently lifts me into his arms. I must weigh double what I did when we first met, so this is no easy feat, yet he carries me down the stairs as if I weigh no more than my ten-pound pup. I nuzzle my nose into his shoulder, breathing in his scent, which I've come to associate with safety and comfort.

My water breaks in the car, a sensation I really don't know how to describe. Becca explained it to me like a bubble popping, but that doesn't quite capture the truly bizarre *emptying* I feel. It's anything but reassuring.

I reach out to grab Grant's hand, who rubs my knuckles comfortingly. He's on the phone, notifying the hospital that we're on our way.

A nurse in scrubs stands waiting outside the emergency room entrance, wheelchair before her. Grant parks the car, walks around to my side, opens the door, and lifts me into the chair in under ten seconds. Then I'm being whisked down the hall, but everything feels like it's moving in slow motion. The colors of nurses' scrubs . . . the sounds of quiet conversations . . . the smell of disinfectant.

All my senses are heightened. But instead of trying to focus on what's happening around me, my attention is on what's happening inside my body.

Grant's hand is on my shoulder, keeping me tethered to the here and now, an anchor in this wild storm. I take a deep breath, trying to stay calm.

And that's when the pain starts.

Oh my God.

I never thought it would be like this. The contractions are brutal now, tearing through me in unrelenting waves. I cry out, unable to contain the sheer panic rolling through me.

"Grant—"

"It's okay, sweetheart. You're okay."

"But I don't know—"

"You're doing everything right. You're in good hands. You're safe. The baby's safe."

With my eyes scrunched closed, I can't process how or when it happens, but somehow I'm on the hospital bed. The nurses hook me up to an IV, trying to keep me still as I writhe in agony. Grant whispers something about an epidural in my ear, and I nod violently.

I hear him speaking to the nurse, and a few minutes later, I'm informed that the anesthesiologist is here to administer the epidural.

Thank you, Lord.

Grant steps back at the nurse's request, and I feel several warm hands turning me onto my side. I open my eyes, meeting Grant's stormy gaze from across the room. He takes a deep breath, encouraging me to do the same. Together, we breathe.

In, two, three, four.

Hold, two, three, four.

Out, two, three, four.

And again.

When the nurses help me lie back, the epidural administered, I feel calmer. More capable. As Grant's eyes lock on mine, I can see the complete trust and admiration in them. He stays by my side as the nurse checks my progress.

"You're dilated to a seven already. Good job. We may be ready to push in another hour or two."

I nod, unsure how in the world I'm going to do this. It's all moving so fast.

Grant stays at my side, stroking my hair, murmuring encouraging things, holding my hand.

Suddenly, I'm so thankful that he's here and not traveling for an away game. I always knew that was a possibility, and told myself I'd be fine with that, that I could handle it. But I know in this moment that was a lie I told myself. I'm so freaking glad he's here.

A little while later, the nurse checks me again and announces that it's time. The doctor is paged, and my hospital room buzzes with activity.

When the doctor enters the room, I don't even have time to get nervous, because suddenly everything is ready and it's go time.

"On the next contraction, I want you to start pushing," she tells me.

I nod, anxious and excited in equal measure. I'm going to meet my baby. *I'm going to meet my daughter.*

Pushing is exhausting. I can't feel anything below my waist, thank God, but these are the longest two hours of my life. I'm quietly sobbing with sheer fatigue by the end of it, sweaty and almost defeated feeling until . . . finally.

One last push, and my baby is here. A tiny, choking cry and an approving nod from the doctor tell me the same thing. *We did it.*

She's placed on my chest, and when I blink away the tears, it's almost impossible to believe this fragile little baby is really mine, that I'm a mother now.

Emotion wells in my throat, and when I look

up to meet Grant's eyes, his are overflowing with tears. I've never seen him cry, and the sight of him so emotional makes my heart squeeze. Watching this big, powerful man practically melt with emotion does something to me.

When the nurses take the baby to clean her off and swaddle her in a blanket, Grant leans over my hospital bed and gathers me in a hug. "You're amazing, Ana. She's beautiful." His deep voice is filled with admiration and awe.

I swallow a fresh wave of tears. "I'm so glad you're here. Thank you, Grant."

He shakes his head. "I wouldn't have missed it for anything."

His statement makes me wonder if he worked out something with his coaching staff about not traveling for any more games until the baby came. But before I can consider it further, the nurse brings my daughter back, and I secure her in my arms.

Grant sits in the chair next to my bed, brushing his calloused fingers against her miniature, flushed ones.

My eyelids are so heavy, heavier than they've ever felt. But every time I drift away, I'm brought back to the faint lights and beeps of the hospital room when a nurse checks on me. I'm beyond tired, and Grant can tell.

He leans across me, pressing a tender kiss to my forehead. "It's okay. You can rest now."

• • •

When I wake from a dreamless slumber, it's not Grant's voice that rouses me.

"Hey, baby girl."

My eyes crack open, just barely, to see my dad standing over me, holding a ridiculously elaborate bouquet. He lays the flowers across my knees and sits on the edge of the bed.

"Daddy?"

"I'm here," he murmurs, and I suddenly feel like an infant again.

Tears roll down my cheeks as I check the room for the real infant. *Where is she?*

"Grant's got her. Don't worry."

Relieved, I sigh, and my dad reaches with cool fingers to wipe my tears away.

"When did you get here?" I ask.

"Grant called after you told him about the contractions. I caught a flight in the nick of time. I've never cursed airport security more, though. Thought I was going to miss it, but here I am. How are you feeling? Are you in any pain?"

"I'm good." I smile and then let out a laugh. "I'm really good."

"Good." He sighs, clearly relieved. "My baby girl's had a baby girl."

"Yeah." I chuckle wetly through my tears. "Weird, right?"

"Not weird at all. Does she have a name yet?"

I think for a moment, biting my lip. I've thought about names a lot. I've thought about strong names, names that will promise to carry my baby into a protected life. Names that will say, *Don't mess with me. My mother raised me to be a warrior.*

"Don't laugh, but . . . Hunter."

My dad reaches for my hand, giving it a gentle squeeze to match the soft wrinkles around his smiling eyes.

"That's a good name. Fierce."

"Right? I think so too."

• • •

Here I thought birthing a child was going to be the hardest part. Little did I know that breastfeeding was an entirely different beast.

Lucky for me, Grant has stayed with me every night since we got the okay to leave the hospital, alternating nighttime feeding duty like a real pro with milk I pumped during the day. If I didn't know for a fact that Grant was a bachelor, I would have certainly guessed him to be a seasoned dad.

A really wonderful seasoned dad.

And even though I haven't told him, I'm so grateful I'm not alone. I wanted to prove to myself that I could do this, but now that seems like the stupidest idea in the world. Of course I *could* if I had to . . . I'm just so glad I don't.

"I've got this one," he murmurs, when we both wake up to the sound of Hunter fussing through the baby monitor on the nightstand. He rolls out of my full-size bed that's too small for him, and stumbles through the dark of the room.

"Thank you." I sigh, nestling deeper under the covers.

"It's no problem," he says, and for once, I believe him.

I can tell that he loves being needed. That he loves both me and Hunter, even if he hasn't said so yet. He once spoke of his dream to be a dad, but I never took him seriously until now.

Grant is an amazing caretaker. He's helped with breastfeeding, with errands and emergencies, cooking and laundry. He's been the one almost exclusively taking care of Hobbes, and with sleepless nights like this one . . .

When Grant snuggles back into bed with me nearly forty-five minutes later, I welcome him with open arms.

"How is she?"

"Just grumpy," he says with a chuckle. "But I held her until she fell back asleep."

"You're the best."

He plants a soft, warm kiss against my forehead. "Get some rest."

And I do.

CHAPTER TWENTY-SEVEN

Bittersweet

Ana

The first few weeks of child rearing prove to be an emotional roller coaster. There are plenty of sweet moments to match the frustrating, exhausting ones. Sometimes I'm impressed with my ability to handle it all. But nothing—and I mean nothing—could ever prepare me for the words that come out of Grant's mouth on this particular evening at home.

"There's something I have to tell you."

His tone is so serious, I find myself suddenly nervous for what he's about to say. I hold Hunter closer to me, her little face tucked away behind a nursing blanket. "What is it?"

"Something happened today. I got a call from

Coach. It's Jason."

What?

"What do you mean? What's wrong with Jason?"

That's a name I haven't thought of in weeks, and what a relief that's been.

Grant plants a hand on my knee, his eyes locked on mine with the promise that he'll be as careful with his words as he can.

Just say it! I want to snap.

"He died."

He . . . what?

"Ana, look at me."

I do, struggling to keep focused on his concerned expression. My mind is racing with thoughts and questions, but I can barely remember how to form words. "What do you mean?"

"He got in an accident. It was a DUI collision."

"You mean . . . he was . . ."

"Yeah."

My heart squeezes painfully in my chest. "Did

anyone else get hurt?"

"No." Grant sighs. "There were some cuts and bruises, but everyone else is alive."

"Well, that's a relief," I say, my voice low and forced. My lower lip trembles as a fat tear drips down my cheek and onto Hunter's forehead. She gurgles, done feeding.

Oh my God . . . Hunter.

"Would you take her?"

"Sure." Grant lifts her small frame from my arms, propping her up against his broad shoulder to begin burping her. "All right, baby girl . . ."

While Grant makes a slow, steady circle around the room with Hunter, I sit with this information. The man I spent years of my life loving, trying to please . . . is gone. Forever.

By the time Grant puts Hunter down to rest, I'm full-on ugly sobbing, grief heaving through my body in sudden, violent bursts. He wraps me in his arms, locking me against him while I struggle to stay grounded.

"I'm— I'm sorry!" I gasp between wails.

"Don't apologize," he murmurs, his breath

warm against my hairline.

"I . . . I just— I feel awful."

"I know, I know."

Sobbing, I choke out, "No, you don't!" How could he? How could he possibly know what this feels like?

"Tell me."

"I don't want to say it." I sniff, trying to pull myself together.

Grant holds me, not pushing me, but not letting it lie either. I need to say it . . . I know I do. I need to get this terrible thing off of my chest. And he knows it too.

"I'm relieved," I whisper, and the weight of a thousand bricks falls off of my shoulders. Despite the tragedy, despite the guilt—I feel so much lighter.

"It's okay, Ana. Whatever you're feeling, you can tell me," he murmurs, still holding me.

I burrow my face into his chest, glad I don't have to meet his eyes when I say this next part.

"You should know. You should know that . . . I think he's the father. I wish it weren't true. I wish it so much. But it's—the calendar." When I choke on the last words, he rubs my back in slow, firm circles, urging me to breathe. "The timing. It's gotta be him. He's her father."

"Ana," Grant murmurs, lifting my chin, and I meet his eyes, barely visible through the tears. "I'm her father. I don't care about biology. I don't care about timing. How could I? I was adopted, right?"

I nod, a hiccup escaping my lips.

"See? None of that matters. I love her. I'll always love her," he whispers against my cheek, wiping my tears away with a sweet kiss. "Just as much as I love her mother."

I lift my face from his T-shirt and meet his eyes.

We've spent weeks working alongside each other, weeks sleeping in the same bed and raising a baby together, doing all the things necessary to run a household, but we haven't talked about *us*. We haven't made love or kissed, or approached the subject of us as a couple.

Grant has comforted me and held me, and changed diapers and cooked and done a million other things, but I didn't know where we stood. I spent practically my whole pregnancy pushing him away, keeping him in a box. I told him I needed a friend, and that was true. But now, I realize, I'm ready for more.

"Grant, I . . ." I pause and lick my lips.

"I love you, Ana."

It's the first time he's said those words to me, and just like that, the walls I spent so long building to protect myself from the hurt that Jason inflicted crumble down.

With a shaky inhale, I lean close and press my lips to Grant's. "I love you too. So much. I'm sorry I've been so stupid, sorry that I spent so much time pushing you away."

He takes my face in his big hands, lifting my mouth to his. "Don't be sorry. You needed time."

I nod. "Kiss me."

And he does, and it's the perfect kiss—slow and sweet and tender. But it's over long before I'm ready for it to be.

When Grant pulls away, there's a serious expression in his eyes.

"What is it?" I ask.

"Are you okay?"

With an inhale, I nod. The news about Jason is devastating, and I feel for his family, but the truth is, I am okay. This entire past year has proven to me how strong I am.

"We need to talk about us," Grant says softly.

I nod. He's right. It's way overdue.

"I'll start," he says. "I'd like to tell you that I'm okay with moving slow, that you can take all the time you need, and we can move at whatever pace you're comfortable with. But none of that would be true."

I swallow. "What are you saying?"

"I don't want to wait, Ana. I want it all. Us living together as a couple. As a family. I love you, both of you, so fucking much. This is all I've ever wanted. And so I hope you don't hate me for pushing, but I gave you space, waited months for you to be ready, and now that we're doing this—I can't wait anymore. You're mine now, sweetheart. Both of you."

"Yes," I manage to say, my voice brimming with emotion.

After that, he just holds me and lets me grieve the loss of Jason in my own way. And when we go to bed that night, we're wrapped up tight in each other's arms. It's the best feeling in the world.

• • •

We don't go to Jason's funeral.

Grant is thoughtful enough to send flowers to the funeral home in time for the service, and a couple of his teammates travel to the funeral. But with a newborn and my own mental health as our priorities, it's better for our little family to stay home.

Over the next few weeks, we're visited by friends—Georgia, Becca and Owen, Elise, Bailey, Sara, and even Jordie. It's a lot of social energy to dole out, but I'm grateful for every congratulatory smile and consolatory hug.

The world keeps spinning, and Hunter keeps growing. With Grant by my side, Hunter in my arms, and Hobbes at my feet, I can't ask for anything more.

CHAPTER TWENTY-EIGHT

Taking Care of Business

Ana

I stand in front of my dresser wearing only a pair of panties as I dig through the top drawer, searching for a bra that will fit. I stopped nursing a few days ago, since I pumped enough milk to get Hunter through another month or so, and then I plan to switch to formula. I'll be going to work soon, just part time, but this seemed like the best option to transition her to.

It's been eight weeks since she was born. We moved back into Grant's condo last month, since it has more space and is much nicer than the apartment I'd rented. Plus, I only had a short-term lease and it was up for renewal soon, so it was the perfect time to go.

Grant wanders into the bedroom, stopping short

when he sees me standing here topless. "I just laid Hunter down for a nap," he says, his voice strained.

"Thanks," I say, rummaging in the back of the drawer where I think I have a sports bra that might work. I packed up all my nursing bras, and none of my old ones fit anymore.

Grant clears his throat, and I glance over at him, stunned for a second by the hungry look on his face. When my gaze lowers, I realize he's as hard as a fence post below the belt, his pants tented out with a bulging erection.

"Um . . ." My mouth lifts in a crooked smile. "Everything okay over there, big guy?"

"Fuck. Sweetheart, can you put on some clothes?" He shifts and adjusts the front of his pants, looking almost like he's in pain.

Realizing for the first time that my post-baby body is still pleasing to him, I feel my heartbeat start to drum faster.

My stomach has flattened out again, and though it's still soft, I've been pleased that I've lost some of the pregnancy weight without really trying. My breasts are still lush, and larger than they were before. For the first time in a very long time, I'm flooded with feelings of desire.

"I was trying to put something on," I murmur, talking a step closer to him. "But nothing really fits."

Feeling bold, I stop just a few feet from where he stands. His gaze tracks hotly over my torso, lingering on my bare breasts. When I cup them in my hands and squeeze, Grant lets out a ragged groan.

"*Fuck*." He breathes out the word, watching me push my cleavage together.

Between midnight feedings, spit-up in my hair, my changing body and hormones, adjusting to motherhood, and moving out of my apartment . . . the last thing I've felt lately is sexy. Which means I have a very neglected, apparently very horny man on my hands.

Suddenly, I feel a little selfish. But it didn't occur to me that just because I wasn't ready for sex, Grant may have felt differently. He never let on. I guess I just assumed he was as tired as me, collapsing into bed each night with sex as the very last thing on my mind. I hate the idea that I've been neglectful. It's time to remedy that.

"You gonna put something on and cover up those gorgeous breasts, or what?" His voice is raspy, thick with unrestrained desire.

"I could," I whisper, slowly dropping to my knees before him. "Or . . ." I unbutton his jeans and slowly pull down the zipper. "We could take everything off together. You said Hunter's asleep, right?"

He nods quickly. "You sure?"

When I tug down his boxers, Grant assists, pushing his jeans down too. They fall to his knees, and I have my mouth on him before he can say anything else. His hands slide into my hair as I welcome the first few inches of him into my mouth.

He hisses out a deep groan.

"Oh, I'm very sure," I murmur with my mouth full of him.

I've missed this. The deep, rumbling sounds that come from his chest. The taste of warm male flesh under my tongue. The dirty endearments he whispers as I suck and nibble on his firm cock.

"*Fuck*, sweetheart. Yes."

"You like that?" I grin up at him, feeling bold and sexy.

He nods, his eyes focused on his cock sliding in and out of my mouth. "Go deeper," he rasps.

I do, and Grant's answering moan vibrates in his throat. It's the sexiest sound.

After a few minutes, he lifts me from the carpet and deposits me on the bed, where he proceeds to make a meal out of me—hungrily licking and sucking on my breasts, then kissing the pulsing spot between my thighs until I'm trembling and very, *very* close to orgasm.

"Grant . . ." I moan, rocking my hips against his face.

"You want my cock, baby?"

I swallow a huge wave of desire and nod.

He joins me on the bed, positioning his big, broad body over mine, and then he's pushing inside, inch by slow inch while I adjust. "Tell me if—"

I cut him off with a kiss. "Don't hold back," I whisper against his lips.

And he doesn't. Moving with such skill and confidence that I'm reduced to whimpering sounds as I cling to his wide shoulders. Fastening his mouth to mine while his talented body wrenches two orgasms from me.

Grant is an amazing lover—generous and decidedly confident. When he gets close, his measured strokes falter and he presses his mouth against my throat. With a low sound, he finds his release, and his cock throbs inside me.

Afterward, he pulls me into his arms and holds me. "That was incredible," he whispers, planting sweet kisses along my temple.

"You looked like you needed that," I say with a grin.

He chuckles. "I really did."

I sit up and meet his eyes. "Why didn't you say anything?"

The doctor cleared me for sex at my six-week exam. Grant knew this. He's known that for a couple of weeks now.

He touches my shoulder, brushing my hair back with his fingertips. "Because you weren't ready. Because I was fine jerking it in the shower every night until you were."

I shake my head at him. "You crazy man. I love you."

"I love you more."

EPILOGUE

Grant

Nine months later

"Well, that's the last of it." Owen dumps a final bag of ice into the cooler and stands back to study his work.

"Thanks, dude." I thump one hand against his shoulder.

"'Course." He grabs a bottle of beer from the cooler, twists off the cap, and offers it to me, then grabs another for himself. "This place is insane, man. Nicely done."

Pride warms me and I tip my chin as we both survey the estate spread out before us. "Thanks." The Mediterranean-style house with white stucco and an orange tile roof came on the market a few months ago, and even though it's more space than we need, I convinced Ana to come and see it.

We'd been living together in my condo, which was great, but I still wanted more space, and a backyard where Hunter could eventually play. We arranged for a private showing with our real estate agent, and Ana fell in love with the place before we'd even made it through the foyer.

Six bedrooms, five baths, a huge chef's kitchen. A formal dining room that we'll probably never use. A home gym, a playroom with all kinds of little built-in nooks and cubbies for toys. And best of all is the privacy aspect.

It's in a gated neighborhood where every lot is at least an acre. Ours has three acres with a private pond in the back. When Hunter is older, I imagine having it stocked with fish and teaching her how to cast and reel. Maybe we'll even get one of those little paddleboats—or a stand-up paddleboard.

Travertine tile covers an expansive pool deck. A hot tub rests under a pergola, complete with a chandelier suspended over it. It's beautiful at night with the soft twinkling lights reflecting off the water.

The place is way over the top. But since I basically went years hardly spending any of my salary, I was able to pay cash for the entire estate. I love knowing that one day, when I'm done playing hockey, even if I retire for good, my family will always be taken care of. And when Ana's dad comes to visit, we'll have plenty of room.

"Seriously, this place is ridiculous, dude." Teddy approaches next, stopping beside us to help himself to a beer too.

"I'm glad you guys could come," I say, changing the subject. I've never been good at accepting a compliment, and there's no reason to start now.

"How many bedrooms does this place have?" Owen asks, unwilling to drop it.

"Six," I say, feeling a little sheepish.

"Better get to work filling those up, Cap," he says with a chuckle.

The idea of Ana pregnant again sends a warm rush through me. As I picture her belly swollen with another baby, and her lush breasts . . . my mouth lifts in a smile. "Yeah, we're working on it. We're waiting for Hunter to turn one before we start trying."

"That's coming up, right?"

I nod. "Next month."

We finished our season last month, and while we didn't set any records, we performed well and held our own in our division. Our coaching staff was happy. And, well, there's always next year.

When Ana had the idea of hosting a combo housewarming party and start-of-the-summer barbecue, I was hesitant at first. But now, seeing everyone here, smiling and playing yard games, I'm glad I agreed.

I used to grumble about the fact I was the loner on the team, recalling all the people who came out for Owen and Becca's baby shower. Seeing that only made me feel more alone and lonelier than if I hadn't been surrounded by a roomful of people at all. Looking around now, though? I'm struck by a deep sense of belonging.

I never imagined I'd be here—hosting a big family-friendly gathering with my wife and baby, and my teammates and their significant others nearby. Kids splashing in the pool. Grill loaded up with enough burgers and chicken to feed an army. Coolers filled with ice-cold beer and organic juice boxes. I smile at the thought of it all. It means even more to me because I truly didn't know if I'd ever get here.

The only person looking out of place is Jordie. He arrived alone, thirty minutes late, and I couldn't help but get the feeling that something was bothering him. He's sitting at the edge of the pool with a beer in his hand, staring off into the distance. I recall him drinking too much at our wedding reception, complaining about his love life and the fact that he's perpetually single.

Deciding that I'll be sure to talk to him later, I cross the lawn to where Ana is standing with Hunter on her hip, talking with a couple of the other hockey wives.

"Hey." She smiles when she sees me.

"Hi, sweetheart." I touch my lips to her neck, unable to resist the temptation to steal a quick kiss.

"Will you take her?" Ana groans. "My arm feels like it's going to fall off."

"We can't have that. Come here, baby girl." I hold out my hands toward Hunter and she babbles something, clapping her hands and grinning her gummy smile at me.

She's been teething lately, and all she wants is to be held. Usually, it's Ana she wants, but sometimes—like right now—I'm lucky enough to be the one she wants.

I hoist her up in one arm, and she settles her little face onto my shoulder. This gets a collective coo of sighs from the women nearby.

"Grant with a baby . . . I don't think I'll ever get used to that sight," Elise says, meeting my eyes with a soft look.

"He's all mine, ladies." Ana's mouth lifts in a smile, watching as I bounce Hunter in my arms.

"As happy as I am to stand here and be objectified like a piece of man candy . . ." I grin at Ana. "Think she's going to make it to lunch, or should I lay her down now?"

Ana reaches over and rubs circles on Hunter's back. "I think she'll make it."

"Burgers are done. Chicken's almost there too."

At this, Hunter lifts her head from my shoulder and makes the sign we taught her for *eat*.

Ana chuckles. "I guess that answers that."

I head back to the grill, and after checking on the chicken, I announce that the food's ready. After I fix a plate for Ana and then one for our daughter, I deliver them to where Ana's sitting in a lawn chair with Hunter on her knee.

"My hero." Ana smiles up at me. "This looks amazing."

"My pleasure." I lean down to take Hunter from her once again so she can eat. "I'll feed her," I say when Ana meets my eyes.

"You sure?"

"Of course. Eat your lunch while it's hot."

Her expression softens, and she shakes her head. "What I ever did to deserve you, I'll never know."

I chuckle. "I think it's the other way around, babe." Then I lean close and lower my voice. "The guys were asking when we're going to start working on filling up some of those bedrooms."

Her eyes flash with heat. "We might be able to work on that . . ."

"Tonight," I growl.

Ana's kissable mouth relaxes, and her eyes crinkle with amusement. "Your daddy is a very naughty boy, Hunter," she says before taking a big bite of her burger.

"Hey, I'm behaving." I hold up one hand in mock surrender. "I could have made some remark

about wishing it was my meat you were biting into
. . ."

"Biting?" She chuckles.

"Good point. Wrong word. Maybe . . . wishing it was my meat you had in your mouth."

She laughs again. "Go get yourself some food. I think the lack of calories is making you delirious."

I chuckle and head off to follow my marching orders. If there's one thing I've learned over the past six months of being married, it's that the phrase *happy wife, happy life* is spot-on accurate. And my main mission in life now is to keep Ana happy. A mission I'm more than good with.

It used to be that all I had was hockey. Now my life is so full of love, and family, and friendships. Ever since I met Ana, not a single day has gone by that I haven't been grateful for her in my life, grateful for the man she's turned me into.

Just as I'm loading my plate with food, Jordie wonders over, looking more serious than I've ever seen him.

"Hey, man, can we talk?" he asks, his voice low.

I nod. "Of course. Lead the way."

• • •

There is one last Hot Jocks novel coming your way. Don't miss Jordie's book with **Taking His Shot**.

HAVE YOU MET ALL THE HOT JOCKS YET?

Hot Jocks Series Reading Order

Playing for Keeps – Justin and Elise

All the Way – Becca and Owen

Trying to Score – Teddy and Sara

Crossing the Line – Asher and Bailey

The Bedroom Experiment – Morgan and Isla – a spin-off novelette

Down and Dirty – Landon and Aubree

Wild for You – Grant and Ana

Taking His Shot – Jordie and Harper

TAKING HIS SHOT

She says she doesn't date players.

She swears up and down that she'll never handle my stick.

We'll see about that, sweetheart.

When I win the pleasure of Harper's company at a charity auction, I get exactly one date—one shot to win over the gorgeous and feisty brunette.

Game on. I play hard, and I love a challenge.

But just when I think I've finally carved out my shot . . . two huge secrets implode around us, threatening everything we've built.

What to expect: A determined hockey player, a hard-to-win-over heroine. Exposed secrets, steamy good times, and a male-only romance book club. Yes!

Note: This is the final book in the Hot Jocks series, but each book is about a new couple and can be read as a complete standalone.

ACKNOWLEDGMENTS

A humongous thank-you to all the lovely readers who have diligently followed this series. I have honestly never had more fun writing about a group of characters, and I *so appreciate* your enthusiasm.

I would like to give a big hug and a sincere thank-you to all of the fabulous book bloggers who continue to share about my books on their social platforms, leave reviews, and post gorgeous Instagram images. Thank you so much!

To my entire team, a massive bear hug. Especially Alyssa Garcia, Rachel Brookes, and Pam Berehulke . . . thank you so much for all your work in helping to bring my books to life. I'm grateful for each and every one of you.

Last, but not least, thank you to my amazing family for your unending support.

CPSIA information can be obtained
at www.ICGtesting.com
Printed in the USA
LVHW090017150420
653368LV00003BA/603